PENGUIN BOOKS

the whole story and other stories

'Smith draws the reader in . . . a joy to read' *Sunday Times*

'Smith proves she has a talent for making the most extraordinary occurrences seem believable, and for finding the extraordinary in everyday events' *Daily Mail*

'Smith's tales are flowing and poetic' *She*

'Smith is strikingly clever. Read her and cheer; you've found a superb writer' *Sleazenation*

'Stunning' *Observer*

'Smith transforms the everyday into the extraordinary' *Elle*

'Few writers are as inventive as Ali Smith' *Red*

'Unsettling and compelling' *Image*

'An exuberant collection of twelve quirky stories, taking us through every month of the year in a celebration of love, life, books and trees' *Daily Mail*

about the author

Ali Smith was born in Inverness in 1962 and lives in Cambridge. She is the author of *Free Love*, *Like*, *Other Stories and Other Stories*, *Hotel World* and *The Whole Story and Other Stories*.

ali smith

the whole story and other stories

PENGUIN BOOKS

PENGUIN BOOKS

Published by the Penguin Group
Penguin Books Ltd, 80 Strand, London WC2R 0RL, England
Penguin Group (USA), Inc., 375 Hudson Street, New York, New York 10014, USA
Penguin Books Australia Ltd, 250 Camberwell Road, Camberwell, Victoria 3124, Australia
Penguin Books Canada Ltd, 10 Alcorn Avenue, Toronto, Ontario, Canada M4V 3B2
Penguin Books India (P) Ltd, 11 Community Centre, Panchsheel Park, New Delhi – 110 017, India
Penguin Group (NZ), Cnr Airborne and Rosedale Roads, Albany, Auckland 1310, New Zealand
Penguin Books (South Africa) (Pty) Ltd, 24 Sturdee Avenue, Rosebank 2196, South Africa

Penguin Books Ltd, Registered Offices: 80 Strand, London WC2R 0RL, England

www.penguin.com

First published by Hamish Hamilton 2003
Published in Penguin Books 2004
4

Set in 12/14.5 pt Monotype Sabon
Typeset by Rowland Phototypesetting Ltd, Bury St Edmunds, Suffolk
Printed in England by Clays Ltd, St Ives plc

ISBN-13: 978–0–140–29680–8

in memory of
Sorley Macdonald

for Kate Atkinson
friend for all seasons

and for Sarah Wood
whole heartedly

acknowledgements and thanks

thank you to the *TLS*, the *Scotsman*, *Chapman*,
Damage Land, *Groundswell*, *Scottish Book Collector*
and all the other anthologies and magazines where
stories from this collection have appeared.

thank you to the Arts Foundation
for their crucial support
and their award of a fellowship
during the writing of this collection.
Special thanks to Alastair.

thank you to the Royal Literary Fund
for sending me on retreat to Ledig House, NY,
where I finished this book.

thank you, Xandra, Kasia, Meg, Ellen and Becky.

thank you, David and thank you, Simon.

thank you, Donald.

thank you, Sarah.

contents

the universal story   1

gothic   15

being quick   27

may   53

paradise   71

erosive   115

the book club   123

believe me   137

scottish love songs   149

the shortlist season   167

the heat of the story   181

the start of things   195

Everything in the world began with a yes. One molecule said yes to another molecule and life was born. But before prehistory there was the prehistory of prehistory and there was the never and there was the yes.

Clarice Lispector

the universal story

There was a man dwelt by a churchyard.

Well, no, okay, it wasn't always a man; in this particular case it was a woman. There was a woman dwelt by a churchyard.

Though, to be honest, nobody really uses that word nowadays. Everybody says cemetery. And nobody says dwelt any more. In other words:

There was once a woman who lived by a cemetery. Every morning when she woke up she looked out of her back window and saw –

Actually, no. There was once a woman who lived by – no, in – a second-hand bookshop. She lived in the flat on the first floor and ran the shop which took up the whole of downstairs. There she sat, day after day, among the skulls and the bones of second-hand books, the stacks and shelves of them spanning the lengths and breadths of the long and narrow rooms, the piles of them swaying up, precarious like rootless towers, towards the cracked plaster of the ceiling. Though their bent or riffled or still chaste spines had been bleached by years of anonymous long-gone light, each of them had been new once, bought in a bookshop full of the shine of other new books. Now each was here, with too many possible reasons to guess at when it came to the question of how it had ended up sunk in the bookdust which specked the air in which the woman, on this winter's day, sat by herself, sensing all round her the weight of it, the covers shut on so many millions of pages that might never be opened to light again.

The shop was down a side street off the centre of a small rural village which few tourists visited in the summer and in which business had slowed considerably since 1982, the year the Queen Mother, looking frail and holding her hat on her head with one hand because of the wind, had cut the ribbon on the bypass which made getting to the city much quicker and stopping in the village quite difficult. Then the bank had closed and eventually the post office. There was a grocer's but most people drove to the supermarket six miles away. The supermarket also stocked books, though hardly any.

Occasionally someone would come into the second-hand bookshop looking for something he or she had heard about on the radio or read about in the papers. Usually the woman in the shop would have to apologize for not having it. For instance, it was February now. Nobody had been into the shop for four days. Occasionally a bookish teenage girl or boy, getting off the half-past four school bus which went between the village and the town, used to push, shy, at the door of the shop and look up with the kind of delight you can see even from behind in the shoulders and back and the angle of head of a person looking up at the endless promise of books. But this hadn't happened for a while.

The woman sat in the empty shop. It was late afternoon. It would be dark soon. She watched a fly in the window. It was early in the year for flies. It flew in veering triangles then settled on The Great Gatsby by F. Scott Fitzgerald to bask in what late winter sun there was.

Or – no. Wait:

There was once a fly resting briefly on an old paperback book in a second-hand bookshop window. It had paused there in a moment of warmth before launching back into the air, which it would do any second now. It wasn't any special or unusual kind of fly or a fly with an interesting species name – for instance, a robber fly or an assassin fly, a bee fly or a thick-headed fly, a dance fly, a dagger fly, a snipe fly or a down-looker fly. It wasn't even a stout or a cleg or a midge. It was a common house fly, a *musca domesticus linnaeus*, of the diptera family, which means it had two wings. It stood on the cover of the book and breathed air through its spiracles.

It had been laid as an egg less than a millimetre long in a wad of manure in a farmyard a mile and a half away and had become a legless maggot feeding off the manure it had been laid in. Then, because winter was coming, it had wriggled by sheer muscle contraction nearly a hundred and twenty feet. It had lain dormant for almost four months in the grit round the base of a wall under several feet of stacked hay in the barn. In a spell of mild weather over the last weekend it had broken the top off the pupa and pulled itself out, a fly now, six millimetres long. Under an eave of the barn it had spread and dried its wings and waited for its body to harden in the unexpectedly springlike air coming up from the Balearics. It had entered the rest of the world through a fly-sized crack in the roof of the barn that morning then zigzagged for over a mile looking for light, warmth and food. When the woman who owned the shop had opened her kitchen window to let the condensation out as she cooked her lunch, it had flown in. Now it was excreting and regurgitating, which is what flies do when they rest on the surfaces of things.

To be exact, it wasn't an it, it was a female fly, with a longer body and red slitted eyes set wider apart than if she had been a male fly. Her wings were each a thin, perfect, delicately veined membrane. She had a grey body and six legs, each with five supple joints, and she was furred all over her legs and her body with minuscule bristles. Her face was striped velvet-silver. Her long mouth had a sponging end for sucking up liquid and for liquefying solids like sugar or flour or pollen.

She was sponging with her proboscis the picture of the actors Robert Redford and Mia Farrow on the cover of the Penguin 1974 edition of The Great Gatsby.

But there was little there really of interest, as you might imagine, to a house fly which needs urgently to feed and to breed, which is capable of carrying over one million bacteria and transmitting everything from common diarrhoea to dysentery, salmonella, typhoid fever, cholera, poliomyelitis, anthrax, leprosy and tuberculosis; and which senses that at any moment a predator will catch her in its web or crush her to death with a fly-swat or, if she survives these, that it will still any moment now simply be cold enough to snuff out herself and all ten of the generations she is capable of setting in motion this year, all nine hundred of the eggs she will be capable of laying given the chance, the average twenty days of life of an average common house fly.

No. Hang on. Because:

There was once a 1974 Penguin edition of F. Scott Fitzgerald's classic American novel The Great Gatsby in the window of a quiet second-hand bookshop in a village that very few people visited any more. It had a hundred and eighty-eight numbered pages and was the twentieth Penguin edition of this particular novel – it had been reprinted three times in 1974 alone; this popularity was partly due to the film of the novel which came out that year, directed by Jack Clayton. Its cover, once bright yellow, had already lost most of its colour before it arrived at the shop. Since the book had been in the window it had whitened even more. In the film-still on it, ornate in a twenties-style frame, Robert Redford and Mia Farrow, the stars of the film, were also quite faded, though Redford was still dapper in his golf cap and Farrow, in a very becoming floppy hat, suited the sepia effect that the movement of sun and light on the glass had brought to her quite by chance.

The novel had first been bought for 30p (6/-) in 1974 in a Devon bookshop by Rosemary Child who was twenty-two and who had felt the urge to read the book before she saw the film. She married her fiancé Roger two years later. They mixed their books and gave their doubles to a Cornwall hospital. This one had been picked off the hospital library trolley in Ward 14 one long hot July afternoon in 1977 by Sharon Patten, a fourteen-year-old girl with a broken hip who was stuck in bed in traction and bored because Wimbledon was over. Her father had seemed pleased at visiting hour when he saw it on her locker and though she'd given up reading it halfway through she kept it there by the water jug for her whole stay and smuggled it home with her when she was discharged. Three years later, when she didn't care any more what her father thought of what she did, she gave it to her schoolfriend David Connor who was going to university to do English, telling him it was the most boring book in the world. David read it. It was perfect. It was just like life is. Everything is beautiful, everything is hopeless. He walked to school quoting bits of it to himself under his breath. By the time he went up north to university in Edinburgh two years later, now a mature eighteen-year-old, he admired it, as he said several times in the seminar, though he found it a little adolescent and believed the underrated Tender is the Night to be Fitzgerald's real masterpiece. The tutor, who every year had to mark around a hundred and fifty abysmal first-year essays on The Great Gatsby, nodded sagely and gave him a high pass in his exam. In 1985, having landed a starred first and a job in personnel management, David sold all his old literature course books to a girl called Mairead for thirty pounds. Mairead didn't like English – it had no proper answers – and decided to do economics instead. She sold them all again, making a lot more money than David had. The Great Gatsby went for £2.00, six times its original price, to a first-year student called Gillian Edgbaston. She managed never to read it and left it on the shelves of the rented house she'd been living in when she moved out in 1990. Brian Jackson, who owned the rented house, packed it in a box which sat behind the freezer in his garage for five years. In 1995 his mother, Rita, came to visit and while he was tidying out his garage she found it in the open box, just lying there on the gravel in his driveway. The Great Gatsby! she said. She hadn't read it for years. He remembers her reading it that summer, it was two summers before she died, and her feet were up on the sofa and her head was deep in the book. She had a whole roomful of books at home. When she died in 1997 he boxed them all up and gave them to a registered charity. The registered charity checked through them for what was valuable and sold the rest on in auctioned boxes of thirty miscellaneous paperbacks, a fiver per box, to second-hand shops all over the country.

The woman in the quiet second-hand bookshop had opened the box she bought at auction and had raised her eyebrows, tired. Another Great Gatsby.

The Great Gatsby. F. Scott Fitzgerald. Now a Major Picture. The book was in the window. Its pages and their edges were dingy yellow because of the kind of paper used in old Penguin Modern Classics; by nature these books won't last. A fly was resting on the book now in the weak sun in the window.

But the fly suddenly swerved away into the air because a man had put his hand in among the books in the window display in the second-hand bookshop and was picking the book up.

Now:

There was once a man who reached his hand in and picked a second-hand copy of F. Scott Fitzgerald's The Great Gatsby out of the window of a quiet second-hand bookshop in a small village. He turned the book over as he went to the counter.

How much is this one, please? he asked the grey-looking woman.

She took it from him and checked the inside cover.

That one's £1, she said.

It says thirty pence here on it, he said, pointing to the back.

That's the 1974 price, the woman said.

The man looked at her. He smiled a beautiful smile. The woman's face lit up.

But, well, since it's very faded, she said, you can have it for fifty.

Done, he said.

Would you like a bag for it? she asked.

No, it's okay, he said. Have you any more?

Any more Fitzgerald? the woman said. Yes, under F. I'll just –.

No, the man said. I mean, any more copies of The Great Gatsby.

You want another copy of The Great Gatsby? the woman said.

I want all your copies of it, the man said, smiling.

The woman went to the shelves and found him four more copies of The Great Gatsby. Then she went through to the storeroom at the back of the shop and checked for more.

Never mind, the man said. Five'll do. Two pounds for the lot, what do you say?

His car was an old Mini Metro. The back seat of it was under a sea of different editions of The Great Gatsby. He cleared some stray copies from beneath the driver's seat so they wouldn't slide under his feet or the pedals while he was driving and threw the books he'd just bought over his shoulder on to the heap without even looking. He started the engine. The next second-hand bookshop was six miles away, in the city. His sister had called him from her bath two Fridays ago. James, I'm in the bath, she'd said. I need F. Scott Fitzgerald's The Great Gatsby.

F what's the what? he'd said.

9

She told him again. I need as many as possible, she said.

Okay, he'd said.

He worked for her because she paid well; she had a grant.

Have you ever read it? she asked.

No, he'd said. Do I have to?

So we beat on, she'd said. Boats against the current. Borne back ceaselessly into the past. Get it?

What about petrol money, if I'm supposed to drive all over the place looking for books? he'd said.

You've got five hundred quid to buy five hundred books. You get them for less, you can keep the change. And I'll pay you two hundred on top for your trouble. Boats against the current. It's perfect, isn't it?

And petrol money? he'd said.

I'll pay it, she'd sighed.

Because:

There was once a woman in the bath who had just phoned her brother and asked him to find her as many copies of The Great Gatsby as possible. She shook the drips off the phone, dropped it over the side on to the bathroom carpet and put her arm back into the water quick because it was cold.

She was collecting the books because she made full-sized boats out of things boats aren't usually made out of. Three years ago she had made a three-foot long boat out of daffodils which she and her brother had stolen at night from people's front gardens all over town. She had launched it, climbing into it, in the local canal. Water had come up round her feet almost immediately, then up round her knees, her thighs, till she was midriff-deep in icy water and daffodils floating all round her, unravelled.

But a small crowd had gathered to watch it sink and the story had attracted a lot of local and even some national media attention. Sponsored by Interflora, which paid enough for her to come off unemployment benefit, she made another boat, five feet long and out of mixed flowers, everything from lilies to snowdrops. It also sank, but this time was filmed for an arts project, with her in it, sinking. This had won her a huge arts commission to make more unexpected boats. Over the last two years she had made ten- and twelve-footers out of sweets, leaves, clocks and photographs and had launched each one with great ceremony at a different UK port. None of them had lasted more than eighty feet out to sea.

The Great Gatsby, she thought in the bath. It was a book she remembered from her adolescence and as she'd been lying in the water fretting about what to do next so her grant wouldn't be taken away from her it had suddenly come into her head.

It was perfect, she thought, nodding to herself. So we beat on. The last line of the book. She ducked her shoulders under the water to keep them warm.

And so, since we've come to the end already:

The seven-foot boat made of copies of The Great Gatsby stuck together with waterproof sealant was launched in the spring in the port of Felixstowe.

11

The artist's brother collected over three hundred copies of The Great Gatsby and drove between Wales and Scotland doing so. It is still quite hard to buy a copy of The Great Gatsby second-hand in some of the places he visited. It cost him a hundred and eighty three pounds fifty exactly. He kept the change. He was also a man apt to wash his hands before he ate, so was unharmed by any residue left by the fly earlier in the story on the cover of the copy he bought in the quiet second-hand bookshop.

This particular copy of The Great Gatsby, with the names of some of the people who had owned it inked under each other in their different handwritings on its inside first page – Rosemary Child, Sharon Patten, David Connor, Rita Jackson – was glued into the prow of the boat, which stayed afloat for three hundred yards before it finally took in water and sank.

The fly which had paused on the book that day spent that evening resting on the light fitting and hovering more than five feet above ground level. This is what flies tend to do in the evenings. This fly was no exception.

The woman who ran the second-hand bookshop had been delighted to sell all her copies of The Great Gatsby at once, and to such a smiling young man. She replaced the one which had been in the window with a copy of Dante's The Divine Comedy and as she was doing so she fanned open the pages of the book. Dust flew off. She blew more dust off the top of the pages then wiped it off her counter. She looked at the book dust smudged on her hand. It was time to dust all the books, shake them all open. It would take her well into the spring. Fiction, then non-fiction, then all the sub-categories. Her heart was light. That evening she began, at the letter A.

The woman who lived by a cemetery, remember, back at the very beginning? She looked out of her window and she saw – ah, but that's another story.

And lastly, what about the first, the man we began with, the man dwelt by a churchyard?

He lived a long and happy and sad and very eventful life, for years and years and years, before he died.

gothic

This actually happened to me.

It was an afternoon in spring not long ago, in the mid 1990s. A man came into the bookshop where I was working. He looked like a bank clerk or an accountant or some kind of businessman; he had distinguished looking hair and was wearing a suit and tie. I straightened my shoulders. I was already in trouble at work and didn't want to get into any more trouble. He looked like he might be important.

I worked in a more old-fashioned bookshop at that time; what I was in trouble for was not wearing the right kinds of clothes. Shortly before the day I'm talking about I had gone to work wearing a sweatshirt with a designer slogan on it. It said across my back IN A DREAM YOU SAW A WAY TO SURVIVE AND YOU WERE FILLED WITH JOY. The sweatshirt had caused a major staff commotion and I had been called to the boss's office and given a dressing down (as it were), a row about always wearing trousers instead of a skirt and thirty pounds' unprecedented allowance to go and buy some proper blouses. There was a lot of anger in the staffroom about me getting money for clothes. The old members of staff, who smoked a lot, thought it was outrageous, though they already thought I was outrageous anyway for not wearing the right kinds of clothes, and the young members of staff, sitting resentful in the veil of thick cigarette smoke, thought that it was unfair and that they should get a blouse allowance too.

I was wearing one of the proper blouses the day I'm talking about. They both itched and I disliked the cowed, dulled person I felt I'd been made to become by wearing them. But I smiled at the man who'd come in. He was nothing like the man standing over there, behind him, at the shelf where The Chronicle of the Twentieth Century was kept.

The Chronicle of the Twentieth Century, until a couple of weeks before, had always been out with its pages open somewhere in the middle of the century on the lectern specially supplied to the shop by its publisher. Three of us worked on the ground floor and we had decided to remove the lectern because every day this man came in, took out his wet handkerchief and hung it over the back of the lectern while he read the Chronicle. Every day the same; he would come in, he would hang it up, read for hours then finger it to see how dry it was, fold it up, put it in his coat pocket and leave the shop.

We were always getting people acting weird in that shop. It had been a bookshop for hundreds of years, in the same old building full of hidden corners, sudden staircases, unexpected rooms. People had died in that bookshop. Old members of staff were always talking, huskily through the breathed-out smoke in the staff-room, about the day one of them found the lady lying dead among her shopping bags, her legs sticking straight out, her coat askew and a look of surprise on her face, or the day another of them found the man sitting on one of the windowsills on the third-floor stairwell staring straight ahead, dead.

We had a man who used to steal books, bring them back again after reading them, slide them on to the shelves and choose new ones to take away with him. We called him the Maniokleptic. We had a man who would fall asleep as he stood leaning against the shelves. We called him the Narcoleptic. We had a woman who would come in and pick up whatever was on the New Books table, turning the pages very fast like she was taking photographs with her eyes. We called her the Critic. We called the two old ladies who always came to any readings at the shop so they could drink the free wine Raincoat and Mrs Stick (Mrs Stick used a stick to walk with). I much preferred working down on the ground floor; where I'd worked first, up in a room off a staircase at the back of the second floor, we were always having to clear up after the people who urinated in True Crime, the spines of Dead by Sunset, The Yorkshire Ripper, Massacre, Crimes Against

Humanity, Perfect Victim, The Faber Book of Murder dripping again under the fluorescent light. We called the urinators the Gothics.

Our name for the man with the handkerchief was Toxic. The day we took the lectern away all three of us gathered at the front desk nudging and shushing each other to see what would happen. He came in as usual. He stood where the lectern usually was. Then he came over to the counter. Barbara stared at the floor. I stared at my hands on the counter. He asked Andrea if she could point him in the direction of The Chronicle of the Twentieth Century.

Andrea blushed. She was the ground-floor sub-manager. She raised her arm and pointed it out to him in Non-Fiction. Then she said, wait. I'll show you. She took him over and found it for him. We all watched him spread the book open on the shelf at reading level, shake his wet handkerchief open and hang it off the edge of the bookshelf; it draped over the books on the shelf below. When it was dry he closed the book, put it back where it came from and left.

He was there again the day I'm talking about. He was always there. I could almost see its contents evaporating into the air, circulating throughout the shop in the ancient rattling heating system (although it was supposed to be spring, that morning there had been a white frost up the sides of all the church spires when I was on my way to work, frost across the endless tenement roofs). Earlier while I'd been watching him

I'd been wondering again about leaving bookselling. I had turned away so as not to have to see him standing in his coat with the grey belt hanging; I looked out of the window instead at the busy Old Town streets and the blackened church and shops, the taxis passing and the wind whipping the people about as they stood by the pelican crossing or hunched themselves against the weather up and down the street where the museum was. My blouse was too tight under my arms. I stretched my shoulders and wondered if the material would rip. I wondered what it would be like to be working at the museum with its glassy-eyed stoats and stuffed hawks and foxes cordoned off behind the Do Not Touch signs, the dinosaur bones wired together the height of the grand hallway, the sound of genteel heels tapping on marble, the scholarly, weighty, methodical air. But they probably had a dress code at the museum too. Probably people like this man would stand about there all afternoon as well, hanging their handkerchieves to dry off the toe-bones of extinct creatures, urinating on the predators. I stood and wondered if there was anywhere in this city I could work where I wouldn't feel that while I was doing it life, real life, was happening more crucially, less sordidly, somewhere else.

Then the smartly dressed man came in and stood at the counter. I smiled at him.

Can I help you? I said.

He put his briefcase on the counter. It was large, old leather, bulging. A businessman wouldn't own such a briefcase; maybe he wasn't a businessman after all. Maybe he was an academic, I thought, since the bookshop is only yards away from the city's medieval university campus, and now that I had thought of him as an academic I could see how his hair was slightly overgrown, how his suit was a little worn and how there was something defensive and clever about his eyes when he looked at me, which he did while he opened his briefcase. It was full of the shining spines of brand-new hardback books. Maybe he was a Christian or some kind of religious bookrep. I frowned.

I am an author and historian, he said. You have probably heard of me. You have almost definitely sold some of my books here already.

He told me his name, which I didn't recognize though I nodded and smiled a suitably respectful smile. It was still mildly exciting when an author came into the shop in those days, the days just before authors were always appearing in bookshops like they are now. Now it is rather mind-numbing always having to associate a face or a voice with a book so that the face and the voice and the name, the body of the writer, are all sold as part of the £9.99 package, tiny peeled slivers of him or her inserted for readers between the pages like erratum slips or bookmarks.

He took one of the books out of the briefcase and put it down on the counter. It had a picture of Hitler on the front. I read its title upside down. It said something about true history.

This is my latest work, he said.

I opened my mouth to redirect him to History. He held up a finger to stop me.

It is the English translation, he said. Because this book is only available in this edition in English, I am having to sell it personally to booksellers and institutions like yours, which is why I am here today in person selling it to you. It will be available, in time, in a more mainstream edition than this one which, as you can see (he turned the spine so I caught a flash of an imprint insignia) has been produced by a small American press. But I would like this book to be available now, sooner rather than later, to all my readers even though it is only at the moment available in this difficult-to-find, difficult-to-order edition. You understand?

I nodded.

I know that a bookseller such as yourself, he said, would like to have all available editions on your shelves as a matter of principle.

He seemed to be waiting for me to nod so I nodded again.

We –, I said.

You see, he said. Much of what reaches us, much of our everyday knowledge, from our knowledge of current affairs to our knowledge of history itself, is heavily censored.

The man leaned forward.

This book, he said, is in its own way a kind of rebellion against exactly what we've been talking about.

He looked boyish, coy. He smiled charmingly.
Censorship, he said, smiling close to my face, is the
death of true history. You could say it's the death of
truth. We are all censored, every day of our lives. You
know what I mean.

Yes, I said.

It is vital that we fight back against this vile
censoring of our identities. For example, he said. I have
been conspired against in all sorts of ways. In fact there
is a conspiracy against me right now. In everything I
do I have to work against others who are working
against me.

He nodded at me now so I would nod back along
with him, which I did, though I had no idea what he
was talking about.

And this means, he said, standing his book on its end
in front of me, that my work is often censored, because
I am writing the true history that no one wants to hear.
I write the truth that a paid conspiracy of Jewish
publishers, bankrolled by a Jewish majority in whose
sole interest the truth is daily denied, will not be
courageous or pure enough to publish.

The man drew breath. His face was slightly flushed. I
was still nodding though I had stepped well back by
now and was scratching my head. I was wondering
where the rest of the ground-floor staff was. There
seemed to be nobody else in the shop, just me, the man
in the suit and the man whose handkerchief was drying
over the books as he read his way chronologically

through The Chronicle of the Twentieth Century.

You see how it is, the man in the suit said. He smiled at me, a winning smile.

I had slid my hand under the counter and had my finger resting on the button we called the panic button which was for when people tried to hold-up the till or for whenever staff felt threatened by anything. But if I pressed it and Security came, what would I say? *This man is a bigot. Please remove him.* Or *I do not agree with what this man is saying. He is a dangerous liar. Please have him ejected from the shop.*

I fingered the button. Um, I said.

He was unloading books out of his briefcase; there were ten or more on the counter.

No, –, I said.

He stopped. He looked straight at me, a book in his hand.

Are you Jewish? he said.

No, I –, I said. It's not –. It's just that I'm not a book buyer. I'm not a manager. You need to be a manager to buy the books in. I can't, I'm just, a, a.

The man looked angry. For a moment he looked vicious. Then his face settled.

I wonder if you might call the manager, he said.

I can call the sub-manager, I said.

Can the sub-manager buy in books? the man asked.

I nodded. I pressed the numbers on the phone. The man and I stood in silence while we waited for Andrea to come down. He looked at his fingernail, rubbed at it impatiently with his thumb. I stood by the till looking hard at the old peeling sticker on its side giving everyone information about how to process barcodes. Andrea came down. She came under the divide and stood beside me behind the counter.

I'm sorry, she said. We don't stock books like yours in our shop.

The man looked almost pleased. Vaguely smiling, he put the books back into his briefcase, closed the clasp and left the shop.

The door swung shut.

Jesus, I said. Christ.

He'll be back in a minute, Andrea said. He always does this. He'll come in the side-door and go up and try History. Bet you a fiver. What did you say to him?

Nothing, I said. I didn't say anything to him.

Then this is what happened next. The man we called Toxic folded his handkerchief up and shut the Chronicle. But instead of going straight out of the shop as usual, he came over to the counter. He stood in front of us and he looked directly at me. He shook his head. Then he looked at Andrea and he tapped the side of his head lightly with a finger, twice. Mad, he said. She's mad, man. Then he left the shop.

When the door had closed behind him Andrea said to me, you know, every time I see that man I'm filled with shame at what we did. Some nights I actually can't sleep because of it.

Then she said, okay, you can go and take your break now.

On my break I was in a terrible mood. The staffroom really smelt of stale smoke. It was a deeply antisocial place. That was the day I decided to make the No Smoking signs and stick them round the yellow walls. It almost caused all-out war.

But soon after the fuss about whether people could smoke in the staffrooms or not, I moved to the new chain down in the New Town. First I helped install the new computers that automatically reorder books which sell more than three copies. Then I was made ground-floor manager. I can wear what I like now (though I am always smart) and I let my staff wear what they like too, within reason.

I have kept an eye out for that Toxic man since I moved. I have never seen him again. We don't get the same kind of person in this shop, I don't know why, other than that it is a clean shop, with wide-open wooden floors and a clean line of books and shelves; and nobody urinates here either, it wouldn't be easy to without being seen. People rarely even sit in the armchairs, because as company policy suggests we leave them in open positions so people won't be comfortable in them for too long. We do have prostitutes; I don't remember there being prostitutes in the old shop. Maybe it was too difficult to negotiate, too obviously nooked and crannied, not open enough to make browsing an innocent-seeming-enough activity. Maybe it was because there was no café at the old shop.

But I tell you. I'm ready. I stand at the counter

behind the computers and I'm waiting. If that man comes in here, if that man ever dares to come in here, I will have him removed. Believe me. I have the power to do it now and I won't think twice about it.

being quick

I was on my way across King's Cross station concourse
dodging the crowds and talking to you on my mobile
when Death nearly walked into me.

I'm sorry, I said.

Sorry for what? you said in my ear. He smiled and
stepped back and stood to one side as if waiting.

I can't stop now, I said, I'm on the phone.

Who are you talking to? you said.

Death was unexpected. He was handsome, balding, a
middle-aged man in a suit so light-coloured it seemed
contrite, and he was vaguely recognizable, vaguely arty,
like a BBC executive from the days when TV still
promised both decency and aesthetic ambition, the
days when its drama was still courageous and you
could trust that the mid-evening news was about what
was actually happening in the world, not ratings or
money or channel protocol. But those days were over
and we both knew it, and anyway I was idealizing

them, his smile, which was melancholy but civilized, said.

He smiled and my phone went dead. I looked at it; its little screen was dark. A moment ago you had been telling me about your day at work and about how you were home now, waiting for me to come home. I had been talking to you about how I was crossing the concourse, how I would probably catch the fast train and be home around eight and how I would get us an Indian takeaway on my way home. We had been discussing onion bhajis.

I gave my phone a shake. Its screen stayed blank. I put it against my ear but there was only the sound of an off phone, the sound of plastic and nothing. I pressed the on button. Nothing happened. I pushed sideways through the crowd to get to the wall of the station and knocked my phone against it, first gently then hard. It made no difference. I looked up, so I wouldn't have to look round, look him in the face. High above the shopfronts and the people milling to and from the trains there was a single strand of some plant or other growing out of the Victorian brick at the top of the wall. It was flowering.

I looked at my phone again. Hello? I said, in case you could still hear me, into the tiny hole in the phone's base.

I started walking. He was walking alongside me, neat and shy. I ignored him all the way round to platforms nine to eleven where I called you from one of the call boxes.

You cut out, you said. Did you want the bhajis or not?

My phone's not working, I said. Listen. Are you all right?

Perfectly, you said. What's wrong with your phone?

Are you sure you're all right? I said.

Yes, you said. Then you said, what? What's the matter? Is something wrong? Are you okay?

He was standing over by the coffee kiosk now. He wasn't looking at me any more; he was looking at a woman and child who were in the coffee queue, at two policewomen wearing luminous yellow and chatting at the platform barrier, at a man asking the people at the cash machines if they would give him their change. I watched him shift his gaze from person to person and knew that even though he was looking at these other people it didn't mean he didn't know exactly where I was.

I told you about him. You laughed.

It's not funny, I said. I'm not making it up. I mean it. He's, like, ten yards away. He's watching the man making the coffee in the kiosk. He's watching him sprinkle on the stuff.

Is it cinnamon? you asked.

I don't know, for God's sake, I said. Now he's watching him fitting the lid on the top. He's watching him do that thing with the napkin that stops the cup being too hot for her to hold.

For who to hold? you said.

The woman, I said, the woman who's buying the coffee.

How do you know it's Death? you said. Doesn't sound much like Death. Sounds like a spy making sure for head office that the kiosk workers are doing everything the way head office requires.

No, no, he's looking at other people too, I said, it's not just the kiosk he's looking at. He's looking at all sorts of people, he's –.

Look again, you said. It's not Death. It's just a person.

I looked again. Sure enough, the man I had thought was Death was an ordinary man, a man behaving a little oddly, but just a man.

You're right, I said. It's just a man in a cream-coloured suit.

How stylish, you said. How springlike. Listen. Call me when you're twenty minutes away and I'll order supper and then you can pick it up and you won't have to wait. Is your bike at the station?

I can't call you when I'm twenty minutes away, I said.

Why not? you said.

My phone's not working, I said.

Oh, I forgot, you said. Okay, how about I phone them when I think you're twenty minutes away? When's your train leaving?

The tinny digital clock ticking over my head said 19:10:53. Then it said 19:10:54. Then it said 19:10:55.

About four minutes, I said.

Good, you said. Run, or you won't get a seat. See you soon.

Your voice was reassuring. 19:11:00, the clock said.
I put the phone back on its hook and I ran.

The seat I got, almost the last one in the carriage,
was opposite a girl who started coughing as soon as
there weren't any other free seats I could move to. She
looked pale and the cough rattled deep in her chest
as she punched numbers into her mobile. Hi, she
said (cough). I'm on the train. No, I've got a cold. A
cold (cough). Yeah, really bad. Yeah, awful actually.
Hello? (cough) Hello?

She looked at her phone as the train went through
a tunnel. So did all the other people who had been in
the middles of conversations up and down the train,
which was packed with people behind me and ahead
of me shouting their hellos forlornly, like lost or blind
people. The stray hellos reached nobody. They hung
unanswered above our heads in the air and cancelled
out everybody they weren't for, then as soon as we
were out of the tunnel the phones began again by
themselves in a high-pitched spiralling, the signature
tunes of TV shows, the simplified Beethoven
symphonies.

The woman sitting next to me was sleeping through
it, her back attentive and straight, a book closed on her
knees and her hands arranged round it. The coughing
girl had closed her eyes too. The man opposite me was
asleep; he had fallen asleep as soon as the train started
to move and was now slumped against the window, his
mouth open in a toothless O. I stared over his head at
the lightly dusked outskirts of London, at its weeds, its

graffiti, its small squares of fast-passing light, the early evening windows of the lives of hundreds of others. I thought how funny it was of me to have imagined that the man who nearly bumped into me was Death. I laughed. The coughing girl opened her eyes and looked at me accusingly. I looked away and smiled to myself, thinking how you and I would joke about it later. I began to think of funny things I could say afterwards, weeks from now, when it had become a running joke. He looked like Death. I thought how the man hadn't looked anything like Death was supposed to look, hooded in black, faceless, with a scythe, standing at the edge of a pond filled with rubbish like on the public information advert on TV when I was small. Then I began to worry in case it was some kind of omen. I told myself not to be so stupid. I drummed my fingers on my leg. They felt numb, anaesthetized, and I knew for the first time as I sat staring blankly out and the real-ization of it broke cold on my skull, for all the world as if someone above me had cracked an egg with a knife and let its cool contents slide out of the shell on to the top of my head and down the back of my neck, that I hadn't ever cared at any point in my life about anything other than myself and that I had no idea how to change this or make it any different.

Then I noticed that the fast train was going very slowly. It slowed to a stop in the dark. This woke several people, many of whom stood up and struggled into coats until they realized they weren't home at all. They sat down again. To the left of us was an Intercity

125, also full of people, also stopped. To the right, another stationary train crammed with people. Someone down the carriage told someone down a phone that we were going very slowly, that we'd stopped, that we were probably passing an accident spot.

A voice came over our speakers. There had been a fatality at a station twenty or thirty miles down the line. All round me people began phoning people to tell them. I got my own mobile out to call you, then remembered and put it back in my bag. Will you tape it? a voice behind me was saying. It's on at nine. Hello? the coughing girl was saying into her phone. Someone died, so we're late.

Just to repeat to passengers, the voice from the ceiling said, and it was a tired and wary-sounding voice. There is as yet no other information. As yet all the information there is is that a fatal incident of fatality has happened on the line, and that no other information has as yet been received, and that more information is awaited, and when it is received it will be told to passengers as soon as it is received.

The man opposite me opened his eyes, sat up surprised, looked out of the window bleary and blinking, closed his eyes again and went back to sleep. The woman next to me had woken up. She settled herself inside her coat and opened her book. It was called Breaking the Pattern of Depression and had been written by a man with a PhD. I glanced at her face. She didn't look depressed at all. She looked perfectly happy. There: I had momentarily cared about someone I didn't know, had never met, would probably never see again after this journey. I looked at the girl, whose eyes were closed again, whose mobile was still in her hand and whose other hand clenched a handkerchief. I tried to feel sorry that she had a cold. Colds were horrible, especially when you had to go to work with one. Her cough was probably keeping her awake late at night. It was horrible to have a cough like that. I looked at the man slumped next to her, big and hopeless as a seal out of water. I had no right to think of him as a seal or as any other kind of simile or metaphor, I thought. I thought kinder thoughts. He must be very tired to be so asleep on a train. Perhaps he had to work very hard. Perhaps when he gets home, I thought, there's something that keeps him awake all night so that the only sleep he gets is on the train. Maybe his wife and he have had a new baby. I looked at his suit. There were no signs of new baby on it. Maybe his wife, or life partner, or whatever he had, was depressed, and it had become an unbreakable pattern. Maybe he or she had a cough that kept them both awake at night. Maybe he lived on his own; maybe he didn't have a wife or a partner; maybe this loneliness was what kept him awake all through the dark hours and meant he could only sleep on trains, on his way to and from work, surrounded by strangers.

I began to feel guilty that I hadn't even idly wondered about the person who had died at the station thirty miles ahead of us. Was it a man or a woman?

How had he or she died? Had he or she had a heart attack? Thrown herself or himself in front of a train on a weekday evening on the mundane journey home, or the journey somewhere he or she couldn't bring herself or himself to make one more time? I had heard somewhere, or read somewhere maybe, that spring was the time of the year when most people found it unbearable, the coming back again of the year's light. Or had it been an accident? Had he or she been running for a train, trying to get home in time? Had one foot slipped off the side of the platform at exactly the wrong moment and the rest of her or him had followed? Was someone expecting him or her home right now, with food in the oven and a TV on, waiting?

I thought of you. You would be imagining me somewhere I wasn't. You would be thinking I was closer to home than I was. You would be phoning the Indian restaurant any moment. Maybe you already had. Maybe you were doing it right now. The thought of you blithely ordering food in the belief that I would be there on time, any minute now, to pick it up; the thought of it cooling down inside its tinfoil cartons in a takeaway bag on some sideboard or other in the kitchen of the restaurant; the thought of you sitting in our front room believing I'd be home any second made me feel worse than any number of imaginings about people I didn't know, even imaginings of them dying.

I got my mobile out but it was still dead. I turned to the woman reading the depression book.

Excuse me, I said.

She looked up.

I wonder if I could borrow your phone, I said.

No, she said.

Oh, I said.

Do you want to know why? she said.

I realized, too late, that she was the kind of person who whispers loudly about rules and regulations at people who eat sweets in libraries.

As a rule of principle, she said, I don't carry a phone.

Ah, I said.

The link between mobile phones and brain tumours hasn't yet been disproved, she said.

Right, I said.

So even if I did carry a phone, I'm not sure I'd lend it to you, she said. By even using one at all, I could be doing not just myself but you and countless others on this train and many hundreds of others I've never met in my life who live near a transmitter serious harm.

Yes, I said. Thanks.

She went back to her book. Her face was shiny with delight. I glanced at the girl opposite. She had one eye slitted open, which she closed quick, in case I saw she was listening. But I'd seen, and she knew it, and opened the eye again.

I'd lend you mine, she said, but there's not enough money left on it for any more calls even if I needed to use it myself. Sorry.

Oh well, I said. Never mind. Nice of you to offer. Thanks anyway.

She nodded and closed her eye. I looked over at the

four people sitting at the table across from us. They all looked away, up at the ceiling or down to the floor or out into the dark at the other people sleeping, reading, on phones, on the stopped trains on the lines parallel to ours, and then our train, which hadn't moved for over three quarters of an hour, jolted to life again and the parallel people in the windows of the trains on either side of us shunted backwards as we shunted forwards.

People up and down the carriage cheered and began to phone people. Good, said the woman with the book. The girl opposite looked at me, looked at the woman reading her book, then looked away to the side as she pressed something on her phone, put her phone to her head and said, in a hushed voice, hello?

We gathered speed. We lurched and rolled on tracks that we knew were precarious beneath us. We slowed down again. People up and down the carriage groaned.

No way, the girl said into her phone, and coughed.

It's like this every bloody time, every bloody time I take a train, a man was saying behind me, probably into a phone but possibly just out loud to himself like a madman. Nobody takes responsibility, he said. Nobody's responsible. Nobody does anything about it. Nobody's in charge. Who's to blame? Nobody.

I saw the scuffed cheapness of the material of the seat I was sitting on. What, I thought, if there was nobody there when I got home? I walked in and you weren't there. I opened our mortgaged front door and came in and took my coat off and sat down with the takeaway bag of food and you weren't there. I didn't take the greasy tops off the cartons, careful not to spill on the floor, while you didn't bring through the plates and forks: you, lifted into the sky like in stories; gone, the way we expect people to vanish into thin air in faked magic, like something only supposed to happen in other people's lives, the lives that don't touch us and our lives. You were gone and the roof blew off our house and left cracked rafters dangling above upturned furniture. The earth below our house broke open and swallowed it whole. I went home and it wasn't there; just a crater in the ground between the other houses, like those old wartime photographs. So someone I didn't know was dead. I didn't care, and why should I? Instead I scared and dared myself into feeling something by imagining what it would be like when what was mine wasn't mine any more, and beyond that was the knowledge, as blunt and undebatable as the glass in the window next to me, that none of it had ever been mine at all.

I looked at my own reflection in it, and through me, behind me, was the dark of the land. It was the end, I'd gone as far as I could go. When the train juddered to a stop at a small station and the overhead voice said we'd be stationary here for at least an hour and a half, possibly for longer, depending on information, and the doors opened and the surge of angry passengers from up and down the train demanding money, taxis, explanations, converged on the one small station manager standing blinking with panic outside his office, I stood up and got off too. I pushed through the people on the platform and followed the exit signs. I didn't know what station or what town I was in until I was outside by the empty taxi rank and saw the name for where I was.

It was a garden city. That was something to do with trees, wasn't it? It meant a city with a lot of trees and green and it meant something historical, but I couldn't remember what. Maybe it stated in its town statutes that there were a certain number of trees that had to be planted here, maybe there was a certain acreage that had to be green; I had no idea, or if I'd ever known in the first place I couldn't remember now.

I looked up the road, then down the road, but I didn't know which was the right way. So I went back in through the station still full of its angry voices. I bypassed the crowd and walked the length of the train I'd just been on, nodding to people I passed who had stepped off for a smoke. We're all in it together, we told each other in shrugs, in little jerkings of the head, what can we do? I got to the front of the train. The driver had his feet up against the window and was reading a paper. I walked what was left of the platform till I'd gone as far as it went. This far along the noise of the station was surprisingly muted. I sat down on the edge then shinned down the side of it on to the track.

It was April, I could feel it. It was slight and cold on the backs of my hands and all through my clothes – my coat was still on my seat on the train. The whole of the lighter part of the year, all the light months, stretched away ahead of me. I put my hands in my pockets and walked, trying to hit a sleeper rung with each step. I avoided the toilet paper and sewage and my feet hurt from hitting the uneven rubble in the dips between the sleepers; my legs already hurt from the short distance I'd come. The rims of the rails curved off ahead of me in what was left of the townlight and the further away from the station I walked the purer the dark beyond me got. Now what I could hear was dark, the passing of cars on roads somewhere in the distance, the occasional rustling of the leafing bushes and the litter on the railway banks on either side of the tracks. I could smell it all, I had cold air in my nose and at the back of my mouth and it tasted of diesel or petrol and behind that it tasted of stripling wood, grass and earth.

I answered it as soon as it rang.

Hello? I said.

An automaton asked me if I would accept a reversed charges call from – and then there was a gap and your voice on the automaton tape, recorded wherever it was you were, saying your name.

Yes, I said, loud and firm in the space left for me to speak into, so there could be no mistake.

Hello, you said.

You were fine. There was nothing wrong with you at all. You were phoning from a call box in an all-night supermarket. You had been on a train that kept stopping because of some kind of accident. You were walking home. You reckoned you were still about thirty miles away. You'd walked on the tracks for hours until three railway workers in fluorescent jackets had run after you, given you a row and threatened to prosecute you. Then you'd walked on the grass verge of a back road and you'd seen the lights of the supermarket across a field. You had mud up round your ankles, all over your shoes and even inside your shoes. You smelt of farm.

I held the phone against my ear with one hand and rubbed my eyes with the other. I was still thinking about your voice saying your name, small and accented and guileless, fastened into the air on the phone tape.

It's surprisingly busy for the middle of the night, you were saying. There are a dozen people, maybe even more, doing their shopping. They're buying, like, Elastoplast, or orange juice. One woman just went through the checkout, she'd come out here in the middle of the night and she bought a child's pair of socks. Why would you buy a pair of socks for a child in the middle of the night?

I don't know, I said.

I really didn't. At that moment I didn't know anything except the small noise of your name. It was the fact that it was just your first name; something about it by itself in all that machinery was making something inside me actually hurt.

I wish I'd asked her, you were saying. She's gone now. I'll never be able to ask her. There's a man over there, his basket is piled completely full of biscuits, they're all the same make, some kind of French biscuit. He told me he drives round all the towns buying this

41

one special kind of biscuit because you can only get them at this chain of supermarket. Amazing what people will do.

Yes, I said. Amazing.

A couple of the people who work here are dancing with each other in the tea and coffee aisle, you said, they've got the radio on over the loudspeakers. And there's boxes of stuff everywhere, they're unpacking it for tomorrow, I mean today, they're putting the things on the shelves. While we're usually asleep someone somewhere is cutting open great big boxes of stuff and arranging them, or cutting bales of new newspapers open for newsagents in supermarkets and shops, and we never even think about it when we buy a paper or whatever.

Uh huh, I said.

It's really interesting being in a supermarket with no actual money to spend, you said.

Yes, I said, I'll bet.

You told me about how you'd left your wallet and your jacket on the train, also the books you'd bought, the work you were bringing home, your glasses and your mobile phone.

It was dead anyway, you said. Though I'll have to try and get the glasses back.

You should cancel your bank cards, I said.

Should I? you said. There's a twenty-four-hour number in the inside of my chequebook, it's up the stairs. But listen, did I wake you? I didn't know what the time was till I got here and saw their clock.

No, it's okay, no worries, I said. Well, you know. I was kind of dozing on the couch.

Oh, and I heard this bird, you said. I was walking along and it was just singing, like they do in the mornings, except that it was completely dark, and there were no other birds singing. I wonder what kind of bird it was. What kind of bird does that, just sings like that in the middle of the night?

Thing is, I said. You'll need to cancel your bank cards and I think it has to be you who does it. I don't think they let other people. If I phone up they maybe won't let me.

I really don't care, you said. I don't care about any of it. Whoever finds them can have them. They can have all the money that's in the wallet. They're welcome to it. It's not as if there's that much left in either of the accounts anyway. Well, except for the one account. Actually, there's quite a lot in that account. Actually, maybe you could phone about that one. The goldcard one. Would you mind? But the other one I don't care about. Oh God. And my credit card. I think my credit card was in there too.

I wrote down the words *credit card* and said that if they wouldn't let me cancel them I'd demand that they registered the loss so you couldn't be charged for anything beyond the time of my calling them up. I looked at the clock. It was ten-past three.

So I'd better go and do that now, I said.

No, wait, you said. Wait a minute.

But that man buying the biscuits. What if he's buying them on your credit card? I said.

I don't care, you said. Don't go. Listen. Can you hear that?

What? I said.

Shh. Listen, you said.

I heard a muffled regular thudding at the back of you like an industrial heartbeat. Possibly this was the sound of my own heart. Certainly something was thudding inside me so hard that I was swaying while I stood in the hall holding the phone.

Can you hear it? you said.

Kind of, I said.

You had started singing along with it. The moment I wake up, you sang. Before I put on my make-up, make-up.

I could hear someone else behind you singing it too.

That's Kerry singing, you said.

Who? I said.

Kerry. She works on the checkout, you said. She's nineteen and has three kids already, all under five, and it's really terrible because she and her husband have to work day and night just to keep their heads above water.

It was quarter-past three on the kitchen clock. You were singing down the phone. I run for the bus, dear. While running I think of us, dear. I realized it was possible that you weren't on the phone at all, that I was just hallucinating that you were. Now you were telling me about Dave, Kerry's husband, who was an apprentice painter and decorator, and how work for painters and decorators was quite hard to come by at the moment because of the boom in DIY.

I interrupted. What happened about Death? I asked.

They stopped the train, you said.

Because of that man? I asked.

Was it a man? you said? Was it on the news? What happened?

Well, you saw him, I said. In the white clothes, at the station.

Oh, you said. Oh, that. I forgot all about that. Honestly. Imagine seeing someone and thinking such stuff. Looked like Death.

You were laughing. I better go and call the bank for you, I said.

No, don't go yet, you said, and your voice was tiny and light in my ear. It's going to be morning soon. The sun'll soon be up.

I know, I said. I've got work in four and a half hours.

Oh. Right. Okay. Quick then, before you go, you said. Tell me. How was your evening? What did you do tonight?

What did I do tonight, I said. Well. First I was torn off the ground with my legs and arms flailing in the air. Like I was a fish on a hook.

Eh? you said.

Like someone in the sky was reeling me in on a huge rod, I said. Or like my middle was tied to a rope and the other end was tied to a plane. And after that, I watched our house collapse in on itself and I spent some time lying in the rubble. Then I vanished completely. I wasn't here at all. Then you phoned.

45

I what? And you what? you said.

I took a deep breath and counted to ten. While I was counting I thought back over my evening.

One. It is early evening. I am lying on the couch watching TV while you come home from London on the train. There's a programme on about a woman who has sent her mother off for the night to pick up the woman's husband, her son-in-law, in Dorset, while some people from the BBC come and secretly remake the mother's back garden. The garden is huge and as they dig up the long green lawn and start laying the slabs that are going to replace it, the TV people keep shaking their heads at the camera about how difficult it will be to do this week's episode in such a short amount of time, especially with the weather being so bad. It rains and rains. There are lots of shots of the TV people and the woman whose mother's garden it is, sheltering under a big old tree. They decide the tree is diseased. In the next shower break they saw through the tree with chainsaws and dig up its roots with a JCB. By the end of the programme the TV people are excited, hiding behind a new pagoda as the woman brings her mother through and shows her the garden, which looks like a modern cemetery. She looks round, bewildered. When the TV people jump out and surprise her she bursts into tears. I can't believe it's really you, she says. I can't believe it's really them. There's a montage of shots of before, during and after. Champagne is opened. The TV people affectionately jostle the woman, the husband and the mother. The mother is still shaking her head, wiping her eyes and staring at the TV people.

The programme finishes. I go through to the kitchen to look at the clock in case the time on the video is wrong.

Two. I phone the restaurant. They tell me I owe them £22.50.

Three. I walk round to the restaurant and pay for the food which I take home and put, still in its bag, in the off oven.

Four. I try your mobile. It passes me through to the answering service. A recording tells me I can leave a message. I leave you a message in which I know I sound slightly high-pitched and strange. At the end the recorded voice tells me I can re-record my message if I press three. I press three and delete my message.

I switch the television back on and lie down on the couch again. Firefighters are at risk from there being too few firefighters. A commercial for Special K. Snooker. A woman saying to a man, I'm sorry, Luke, I really am. A footballer is appealing against a ban for using steroids. The answer is Gormenghast. An old EastEnders in which everyone looks younger and the clothes look dated. Of one hundred people who were asked to name a kind of animal featured in children's stories, no one has answered elephant; a man's family loses a life when he answers elephant. A cartoon. A football match between someone and Brazil. A photograph of a bridge in a village a hundred years ago, a voiceover saying, in those days there were no cars in my grandmother's village. A boyband. A commercial for Kalms. An old Star Trek. A baseball team wants to change the name of its playing field. The weather tonight (clear). Heart-shaped bakeware for sale. An old Coronation Street in which everyone looks younger and the clothes look dated. Jerry Springer saying to an old man with one leg, so you met her in a convenience store? A commercial for digital TV. A: Morecambe and Wise, B: Mulder and Scully or C: Bonnie and Clyde. A glowing brain and a voiceover saying, I think there really is no inner conscious self. All we are is a machine built by genes. An idea can affect your mind like a germ, a parasite. We are the creations of our genes and our memes. I begin at the beginning of the channels again and it is like watching thrown-away rubbish come bobbing in towards me on a tide, stuff that has floated in from all over the world made of substances that will never decompose.

Five. I switch the television off. I go through to the kitchen and try your mobile. The voice tells me to leave you a message. I leave a steady-sounding message saying I hope you're all right and asking you to call me.

Six. I go upstairs and look out the front window. I come downstairs and try your mobile again. The voice tells me to leave you a message. I leave one which sounds much less steady than the last and regret not deleting it as soon as I've put the phone down. I get my own mobile out and text you. WHR R U? XXX. I press send. Message fails. I press send again. Message fails again. I phone 453 and an automaton tells me I have 6p left on my phonecard.

Seven. I open the front door. I stand in the middle of the road and check. I walk along a little so I can see all the way to the corner. I walk to the corner so I can see down the other road. I go back to the house. Light is blazing out of the open front door. I go straight through to the phone in the kitchen and try your mobile. While I'm listening to the voice telling me to leave you a message I remember: you told me your mobile isn't working.

Eight. You are lost. You've got lost somewhere. You don't know where you are.

I stand in the kitchen next to the fridge and pray, which is something I haven't done for years. It's so long since I've done it that I can't really remember how to. I am polite and desperate.

You are somewhere I can't reach or hear you and you are in pain.

I bargain. I promise to become a Catholic again if you will be returned safe.

You are somewhere you don't want me to know about, with someone you don't want me to know about.

Nine. I sit on the couch. I look at my fingernails. Then I look at my thumbnails, first one and then the other. I wonder what would happen if I didn't have a nail on my thumb, or on this first finger, or this little finger. I know it is supposed to be excruciatingly painful, used as a method of torture. We have fingernails, as I probably know from watching something on television once, left over from Neanderthal and animal claws; they protect the nerves in our fingers and are made of protein, keratin. They grow quite fast, quite a lot per week. They even grow for a while after death, and the hair. It keeps growing regardless. Everybody knows this.

I think about how at one point a couple of years ago you tried to stop biting your nails so short by only letting yourself bite one nail a day, the thumb on Monday, the first finger on Tuesday, the next on Wednesday. I try to remember whether you are still doing this or whether these days you just bite any old nail, or whether you don't bite them at all any more. I can't remember. I don't know how long or short your nails are.

Ten.

You were saying my name again down the supermarket phone. Hello? you said. Love? Are you still there?

Yes, I said.

What was it you did tonight? you said.

Oh, the usual, I said. Listen. Do you want me to come and pick you up in the car? It'd only take half an hour.

No, you said. I really want to walk. It'll be light soon, too.

It would; it was April. After we hung up, I would phone the bank, lock all the doors, clean my teeth and go to bed, set the alarm for four hours away, lie on my

back on my side of the bed and try to sleep through
what time there was left with your pillow over my eyes
to keep the light out.

I'll go and phone the bank for you, I said.

Don't go yet, though, you said.

I looked at the clock.

Five more minutes? you said.

Okay, I said.

may

I tell you. I fell in love with a tree. I couldn't not. It was in blossom.

It was a day like all the other days and I was on my way to work, walking the same way as usual between our house and the town. I wasn't even very far from home, just round the corner. I was looking at the pavement and wondering as I walked whether the local council paid someone money to go walking around looking at the ground all day for places where people might trip. What would a job like that be advertised as in the paper, under what title? Inspector of Pavements and Roads. Kerb Auditor. Local Walkways Erosion Consultant. I wondered what qualifications you would need to be one. On a TV quiz show the host would say, or at a party a smiling stranger would ask, and what do you do? and whoever it was would reply, actually I'm an Asphalt Observance Manager, it's very good money, takes a great deal of expertise, a job for life with excellent career prospects.

Or maybe the council didn't do this job any more. Probably there was a privatized company who sent people out to check on the roads and then report back the findings to a relevant council committee. That was more likely. I walked along like that, I remember, noting to myself in my head all the places I would report which needed sorting, until the moment the ground ahead of me wasn't there any more. It had disappeared. At my feet the pavement was covered with what looked like blown silk. It was petals. The petals were a beautiful white. I glanced up to see where they'd come from, and saw where they'd come from.

A woman came out of a house. She told me to get out of her garden. She asked was I on drugs. I explained I wasn't. She said she'd call the police if I wasn't gone the next time she looked out of her window and she went back inside the house, slamming her door. I hadn't even realized I was in someone's garden, never mind that I'd been there for a long enough time for it to be alarming to anybody. I left her garden; I stood by the gate and looked at the tree from the pavement outside it instead. She called the police anyway; a woman and a man came in a patrol car. They were polite but firm. They talked about trespassing and loitering, took my name and address and gave me a warning and a lift home. They waited to see that I did have a key for our house, that I wasn't just making it up; they waited in their car until I'd unlocked the door and gone inside and shut it behind me; they sat outside the house not moving, with their engine going, for about ten minutes before I heard them rev up and drive away.

I had had no idea that staring up at a tree for more than the allotted proper amount of time could be considered wrong. When the police car stopped outside our house and I tried to get out, I couldn't – I had never been in a police car before and there are no handles on the insides of the doors in the back – you can't get out unless someone lets you out. I thought at first I wasn't able to find the handle because of what had happened to my eyes. They were full of white. All I could see was white. The thing with the woman and the police had taken place to me through a gauze of dazed white with everyone and everything like radio-voice ghosts, a drama happening to someone else somewhere at the back of me. Even while I was standing in the hall listening for them to drive away I still couldn't see anything except through a kind of shifting, folding, blazing white; and after they'd gone, after quite a while of sitting on the carpet feeling the surprising hugeness of the little bumps and shrugs of its material under my hands, I could only just make out, through the white, the blurs which meant the edges of the pictures on our walls, the pile of junk mail on the hall table and the black curl of the flex of the phone on the floor beside me.

I thought about phoning you. Then I thought about the tree. It was the most beautiful tree I had ever seen. It was the most beautiful thing I have ever seen. Its blossom was high summer blossom, not the cold early spring blossom of so many trees and bushes that comes in March and means more snow and cold. This was blue-sky white, heat-haze white, the white of the sheets that you bring in from the line in the garden dry after hardly any time because the air is so warm. It was the white of sun, the white that's behind all the colours there are, it was open-mouthed white on open-mouthed white, swathes of sweet-smelling outheld white lifting and falling and nodding, saying the one word yes over and over, white spilling over itself. It was a white that longed for bees, that wanted you inside it, dusted, pollen-smudged; it was all the more beautiful for being so brief, so on the point of gone, about to be nudged off by the wind and the coming leaves. It was the white before green, and the green of this tree, I knew, would be even more beautiful than the white; I knew that if I were to see it in leaf I would smell and hear nothing but green. My whole head – never mind just my eyes – all my senses, my whole self from head to foot, would fill and change with the chlorophyll of it. I was changed already. Look at me. I knew, as I sat there blinking absurdly in the hall, trying to simply look, holding my hand up in front of my eyes and watching it moving as if it belonged to someone else, that I would never again in my whole life see or feel or taste anything as beautiful as the tree I'd finally seen.

I got to my feet by leaning against the wall. I fumbled through thin air across to the stairs and reached out for the banister. I got to the top, crawled from the landing into our bedroom and made myself lie down on the bed and shut my eyes, but the white was still there, even behind the shut lids. It pulsed like a blood-beat; dimmer and lighter, lighter and dimmer. How many times had I passed that tree already in my life, just walked past it and not seen it? I must have walked down that street a thousand times, more than a thousand. How could I not have seen it? How many other things had I missed? How many other loves? It didn't matter. Nothing else mattered any more. The buds were like the pointed hooves of a herd of tiny deer. The blossom was like – no, it was like nothing but blossom. The leaves, when they came, would be like nothing but leaves. I had never seen a tree more like a tree. It was a relief. I thought of the roots and the trunk. I thrilled to the very idea that the roots and the trunk sent water up through the branches to the buds or blossom or leaves and then when it rained water came back through the leaves to be distributed round the tree again. It was so clever. I breathed because of it. I blessed the bark that protected the spine and the sap of the tree. I thought of its slender grooves. I imagined the fingering of them. I thought of inside, the rings going endlessly round, one for every year of its life and all its different seasons, and I burst into tears like a teenager. I lay on my back in the bed and cried, laugh-ing, like I was seventeen again. It was me who was like something other than myself. I should have been at work, and instead I was lying in bed, hugging a pillow, with my heart, or my soul, or my mind or my lungs or whatever it was that was making me feel like this, high and light; whatever it was had snapped its string and blown away and now there it was above me, out of my reach, caught in the branches at the top of a tree.

I fell asleep. I dreamed of trees. In my dream I had climbed to a room which was also an orchard; it was at the very top of a massive old house whose downstairs was dilapidated and peeling and whose upstairs was all trees. I had climbed the broken dangerous stairs past all the other floors and got to the door of the room; the trees in it were waiting for me, small and unmoving under the roof. When I woke up I could see a lot more clearly. I washed my face in the bathroom, straightened my clothes. I looked all right. I went down to the kitchen and rooted through the cupboard under the sink until I found your father's old binoculars in their leather case. I couldn't make it out from the bathroom window or from either of the back bedroom windows but from up in the loft through the small window, if I leaned out at an angle so the eaves weren't in the way, I could easily see the white of the crown of it shimmering between the houses. If I leaned right out I could see almost the whole of it. But it was tricky to lean out at the same time as balancing myself between the separate roof struts so I fetched the old board we'd used under the mattress in the first bed from the back of the shed, sawed it into two pieces so I could get it through the loft hatch, then went back down to the shed, found the hammer and some nails and nailed the pieces of board back together up in the loft.

Birds visited the tree. They would fly in, settle for a moment, sometimes for as long as a minute, and they would fly off again. They came in ones and twos, a flutter of dark in the white. Or they would disappear into the blossom. Insects, which are excellent food for birds, tend to live on the trunks and the branches of trees. Ants can use trees as the ideal landscape for ant-farms, where they breed and corral and fatten up insects like aphids and use them for milk. (I found these things out later that evening on the internet.) Traffic drove unnoticing past the tree. People passed back and fore behind it. Mothers went past it to fetch children from school, brought them home from school past it the other way. People came home from work all round it. The sun moved round it in the sky. Its branches lifted and fell in the light wind. Petals spun off it and settled on a car or a lawn or fell maddeningly out of range where I couldn't see them land. Time flew. It really did. I must have watched for hours, all afternoon, until you were suddenly home from work yourself and shouting at me for being up in the loft. I came down, went online and typed in the word *tree*. There was a lot of stuff. I came off when you called me for supper, then went back on again after supper and came off again when you told me that if I didn't come to bed immediately so you could get some sleep then you would seriously consider leaving me.

I woke up in the middle of the night furious at that woman who thought she owned the tree. I sat straight up in the bed. I couldn't believe how angry I was. How could someone think they had ownership of something as unownable as a tree? Just because it was in her garden didn't mean it was hers. How could it be her tree? It was so clearly my tree.

I decided I would do something; I would go round now in the dark and anonymously throw stones at her house, break a window or two then run away. That would show her what she didn't own. That would serve her right. It was quarter to two on the alarm. You were asleep; you turned and mumbled something in your sleep. I got out carefully so as not to disturb you and took my clothes to the bathroom so my putting them on wouldn't wake you.

It was raining quite heavily when I went out. I scouted about in our back garden under our trees for some good-sized stones to throw. (It wasn't that our own trees were any less important than the tree I'd seen; they were nice and fine and everything; it was simply that they weren't it.) I found some smooth beach stones we'd brought back from somewhere and put them in my jacket pocket and I went out the back way so you wouldn't hear anything at the front. On my way round to the woman's house there was a skip at the side of the road; someone was putting in a drive-way, digging up a front porch. There were lots of pieces of brick and half-brick in the skip and a lot of smashed-up thrown-away paving slab. Nobody saw me. There was nobody at all on the street, on any of the streets, and only the very occasional light in a window.

When I got to the woman's house it was completely in darkness. I was soaked from the rain and there were the petals plastered wet all over the pavement outside her garden gate. I tucked my piece of slab under my arm, soundlessly opened the gate. I could have been a perfect burglar. I crossed her lawn soundlessly and I stood under the tree.

The rain was knocking the petals off; they dropped, water-weighted and skimpy, into a circle of white on the dark of the grass round the edge of the dripping tree. The loaded branches magnified the noise; the rain was a steady hum above me through which I could hear the individual raindrops colliding with the individual flowers. I had my breath back now. I sat down on the wet grass by the roots; petals were all over my boots and when I ran my hand through my hair petals stuck to my fingers. I arranged my stones and half-bricks and my slab in a neat line, ready in case I needed them. Petals stuck to them too. I peeled a couple off. They were like something after a wedding. I was shivering now, though it wasn't cold. It was humid. It was lovely. I leaned back against its trunk, felt the ridges of it press through my jacket into my back and watched the blossom shredding as the rain brought it down.

You sit opposite me at the table in the kitchen and tell me you've fallen in love. When I ask you to tell me about whoever it is, you look at me, reproachful.

Not with *someone*, you say.

Then you tell me you're in love with a tree.

You don't look at all well. You are pale. I think maybe you have a fever or are incubating a cold. You toy with the matting under the toaster. I pretend calm. I don't look angry or upset at all. I scan the line of old crumbs beneath the matting, still there from god knows how many of our breakfasts. I think to myself that you must be lying for a good reason because you never usually lie, it's very unlike you to. But then recently, it's true, you have been very unlike yourself. You have been defiant-looking, worried-looking and clear-faced as a child by turns; you have been sneaking out of bed and leaving the house as soon as you think I'm asleep, and you keep telling me odd facts about seed dispersal and reforestation. Last night you told me how it takes the energy of fifty leaves for a tree to make one apple, how one tree can produce millions of leaves, how there are two kinds of wood in the trunk of a tree, heartwood and sapwood, and that heartwood is where the tree packs away its waste products, and how trees in woods or groves that get less sunlight because they grow beneath other trees are called understory trees.

I fell in love with a tree. I couldn't not. I am perfectly within my right to be angry. Instead, I keep things smooth. There's a way to do this. I try to think of the right thing to say.

Like in the myth? I say.

It's not a myth, you say. What myth? It's really real.

Okay, I say. I say it soothingly. I nod.

Do you believe me? you say.

I do, I say. I sound as if I mean it.

It takes a little while before I do actually believe that it's all about a tree and of course, when I do allow myself to, I'm relieved. More, I'm delighted. All these years we've been together and my only real rival in all this time doesn't even have genitals. I go around for quite a while smiling at my good luck. A tree, for goodness sake, I laugh to myself as I pay for a bag of apples in the supermarket or pull the stick out of a cherry, flick the stick away, toss the cherry in the air and catch it in my mouth, pleased with myself, hoping someone saw.

I am such an innocent. I have no idea.

This is what it takes to make me believe it. I come home from work a couple of days later and find you gouging up the laminate in the middle of the front room with a hammer and a screwdriver. The laminate cost us a fortune to put down. We both know it did. I sit on the couch. I put my head in my hands. You look up brightly. Then you see my face.

I just want to see what's underneath, you say.

Concrete, I say. Remember when we moved in and before there was a floor there was the concrete, and it was horrible, and that's why we put the flooring down?

Yes, but I wanted to know what was under the concrete, you say. I needed to check.

And how are you going to get through the concrete? I say. You'll never do it with a screwdriver.

I'm going to get a drill from Homebase, you say. We need a drill anyway.

You sit beside me on the couch and you tell me you are planning to move the tree into our house.

You can't keep a tree in a house, I say.

Yes, you can, you say. I've looked into it. All you have to do is make sure that you give it enough water and that bees can pollinate it. We would need to keep some bees as well. Would that be okay?

What about light? I say. Trees need light. And what about its roots? That's why people cut trees down, because the roots of them get under the foundations of houses and are dangerous and pull them up. It's crazy to actually go out of your way to pull up the foundations of the house you're living in. No?

You scowl beside me.

And what kind of a tree is it? I ask.

Don't what kind of tree me, you say. I've told you, it's irrelevant.

I haven't actually been permitted to see this famous tree yet; you are keeping it a secret, close to your heart. I know it's situated somewhere over the back since that's the way the loft window faces and you are spending all the daylight hours that you're home in the loft. I know it's just come into leaf and that before, when you first saw it, it was blossoming, all that stuff about it being white, I've heard it several times now, how you were going to phone me but you couldn't see anything but it, etc. Every night in bed before I pretend to go to sleep it's been you telling me more and more things about trees as if desperate to convince me; on the first night I asked you what kind it was and you went into a huff (probably, I thought myself, because in your subterfuge, your attempt to screen your affair or whatever it is from me, you'd simply forgotten to pick a kind and I'd caught you out); because what kind it is, you said, waving your arms about in a pure show of panic, is just a random label given by people who need to categorize things, people are far too hung up on categorization, the point about this is that it can't be categorized, it's the most beautiful tree I've ever seen, that's all I know and all I need to know, I don't need to give it a name, that's the whole point, you said, don't you see?

No, I say, sitting calm and reasonable in front of the wreckage of our room. Listen, what I mean is. Some trees can be kept inside and others can't. It'd stunt them. They would die. And it sounds to me from your description and everything, though I haven't seen it myself as you know, but it does sound to me as if your tree is too big for the inside of a house already.

I know, you say. You drop the screwdriver on the undamaged bit of floor at our feet and you lean into me, miserable. I can sense triumph. You are warm under my arm. I shake my head. I keep my sad face on as if I understand.

And probably its roots are too settled now to move it without doing damage, I say.

I know, you say, defeated. I was wondering about that.

And anyway, I go on, but gently, because I know the effect it will have. The thing about your tree is, it belongs to someone else. It's not your tree to take. Is it?

Probably I shouldn't have said that, though it was worth it to find myself holding you so close later that night, a night you didn't leave me, weren't cold and wooden to me. Certainly it is one of the reasons I have to go and fetch you out of the police station the next day where you are being questioned about wilful damage to someone else's property. I've done nothing wrong, you keep telling me all the way home. You say it over and over, and you tell me it's what you repeatedly told the man recording you saying it in the interview room. I notice that you want to go the long way home, that you're keen not to take the shortcut. Once I've settled you in the house, up in the dangerous loft again with a cup of tea I've made you, I sneak out. I head for the streets you didn't want us to walk down. At first nothing is out of place. Then outside a house on a well-to-do street I know I've found it when I look down and see that someone has written, quite large, on the pavement in bright green paint, the words: PROPERTY IS THEFT.

There is a tree in the garden. I look hard at it. But it is just a tree; it's nothing more than a tree, it looks like any old tree, with its early-evening mayflies hovering near it in the shafts of low sun, its leaves pinched and new and the grass beneath it patchy and shadowed. I can feel myself getting angry. I try to think of other things. I tell myself that the correct term for mayflies is ephemeroptera; I remember from university, though I can't think why or how I ever learned such a fact, especially I can't think why I would have retained it until now. There they are regardless, whatever they're called, annoyingly in the air. For an instant I hate them. I fantasize about spraying them all with something that would get rid of them. I think about taking an axe to the tree. I think about the teeth of saws and of the sawdust the different kinds of wood behind its bark would make.

I wonder if an anonymous letter to the person who owns this house about its dangers to the foundations (though it is nowhere near the foundations) might make him or her consider removing it. Dear Sir, I imagine myself typing, before I shake my head at myself and turn to go and as I do I see the words again on the pavement. The way they're scrawled, how fast and sloping and green their letters are, reminds me of you when we first knew each other, when we were still not far past adolescence ourselves, still knew we'd alter the world.

A woman comes out of the front door of the house. She clearly wants me to stop laughing outside her house. She shouts at me to go away. She says if I don't she'll call the police.

I go home. You're up in the loft. I worry about you up there. It has no floor and you're balancing, passionate, on nothing but thin wood. I imagine you seeing the tree through the thick circles of magnifying glass in the binoculars I used to play with when I was a child; inside your head the tree is close-up, silent, there but untouchable, moving, like super-8 film. I know

you; you never compromise; there's no point in calling
you down. But you've left me some Greek salad on a
plate covered by another plate in the kitchen, a fork
neatly beside it. I sit on the couch in front of the dug-up
laminate and while I'm eating I remember the story
about the old couple who are turned into two trees;
they let the strangers who knock at the door into their
house then find that the gods have visited, and their
favour is granted them. I search around in the books
until I find the book, but I can't find the story about the
old couple in it. I find the one about the grieving youth
who becomes a tree, and the jealous girl who inadvert-
ently causes the death of her rival and is turned into a
shrub, and the boy who plays such beautiful music in
the open air that the trees and bushes pick their roots
up and move closer, making a shady place for him to
play, and the god who falls in love with the girl who
doesn't want him, who's happy without him, and who,
when he chases her, is an exceptionally fast runner,
being such a good huntress, that she almost outruns
him. But since he's a god and she's a mortal she can't,
and as soon as she knows her strength is waning and
he's going to catch her up and have her, she prays to
her father, the river, to help her. He helps her by
turning her into a tree. All of a sudden her feet take
root. Her stomach hardens into bark. Her mouth seals
up and her face mosses over; her eyes seal shut behind
lichen. Her arms above her head grow shoots and
hundreds of leaves spring out of each finger.

I fold down the page at this story. I get some work

things ready for tomorrow and call you, tell you as usual that I'm off to bed, that if you don't come now so I can put the lights out and get some sleep I'm going to leave you.

When we're in bed I hand you the book, open at the story. You read it. You look pleased. You read it again, leaning over me to catch the light. I read my favourite bit over your shoulder, the bit about the shining loveliness of the tree, and the god, powerless, adorning himself with its branches. You fold the page down again, close the book and put it on the bedside cabinet. I switch the light off.

As soon as you think I'm asleep, when I'm breathing regularly to let you believe I am, you get up. After I hear the gentle shutting of the door, I slide myself out of bed and into my clothes and I go downstairs and out the back door too. This first night I wish I'd pulled on a thicker jacket; in future I will know to.

When I get to the house with the tree I see you there in the dark under it. You are lying on your back on the ground. You look like you're asleep.

I lie down next to you under the tree.

paradise

The good people of the town are asleep in their beds.
The bad people of the town are asleep in their beds.
The tourists are asleep in their bed-and-breakfast beds
in the town's bigger houses on the more genteel streets
with their scent of high fir hedge, average price per
person per night between £20 and £30, higher for en
suite, higher for a guest house, a good bit higher for a
hotel. Out down the empty loch road, and the monster
deep asleep in the bed of the loch, the hills and the sky
are beginning to appear again upside down in the
water. It is half-past two in the morning and it is light.

Not that the light ever really went away; between
eleven last night and two this morning the thin line of
blue, which in midsummer means dark, never quite
settled on any of the horizons round the town, and this
is tourist heaven now regardless of foot-and-mouth,
this is the place which will be reported later this year
in the broadsheets as the biggest grossing tourist

attraction in the UK because of its splendid scenery, its welcoming folk, its clean air and its light like this in the middle of the night, mundane and uncanny, prowling out as only light can, the big-pawed hulk of it unstoppable over the fields and the single track roads and the disinfected cordoned-off woods; unstoppable round and behind and over the out-of-town tree that not many tourists ever know about or find, the one by the well at the side of a back road, whose branches and trunk and roots have been hung (and all the other branches for yards around it in the roadside wood, all weighed down too) with the rags from shirts, coats, underwear, skirts, curtains, anything that can be ripped, and socks, hats, handkerchieves, scarves, things left by people making wishes they think will have more chance of coming true if they've ripped something up, something close to them, something they wear or something someone they love wears, and taken it there and hung it on a tree.

The woods are deserted. There is nobody on the road. The rags sway slightly, like terrifying leaves.

Across the farmland, over the firth and down into the town there is nothing but the noise of wakened birds. At the top of the birdsung High Street, inside the concrete box put there by the police, which, when locked from the inside, has no way in from the outside, the boy who's been curled on its floor since three men he didn't know chased him down the road after the club shut, all of them after him along the late night pavements and past the multi-storey and the night-blank shops and across the pedestrian precinct shouting how they were going to beat him to fucking death, standing round the security box kicking its door and battering it, breaking what sounded like bottles on it, then everything going quiet, and then the noise of birds, has stopped shaking and has finally fallen asleep. Inside the box it is always light. The light in there is vandal-proof. On the wall there's a screen and a button for audio/visual communication with a police control room and the boy, who knows better than to ever press such a button, is asleep below the screen, hunched up against the wall of the box with his arm over his eyes.

On the pavement by the door of the box the broken glass is glinting. Up above the town early morning seagulls glint their white underbellies as they cross the sky, and the roofs of houses and the steeples of churches glint, and down there the black river glinting; not yet three a.m. and it's light as daylight now over the town flanked by its new supermarkets, nestled in the curve between its bridge from south to north and its hospital and its cemetery where, the story goes, years ago two men once spent a Saturday night against the gravestones getting drunk, and just when they'd run out of drink a door handily opened in the side of the hill and in they went to a room whose walls were tall, made of packed earth with torches of burning peat stuck in them for light, and there were huge vats of whisky and beer and it was all free, and they had a great time carousing all night with the young and happy well-dressed strangers clinking their mugs and glasses, and

were pretty pleased with themselves for finding a new
pub and making such grand new friends until all
at once without any warning the great turf door flung
itself open again and the hill flung them out, sober, into
the light of morning, and since it was a Sunday they
made their way into town to go to church. But the
town was changed, it was new, things were unrecog-
nizable, and it was when they got to the church, as they
walked together up the aisle past the pews packed with
strangers, good townspeople who had been in their
beds asleep all night, that the two men crumbled away
from the head down till nothing was left of them but
two smoking piles of ash on the stone floor of the
church, and that'll teach them not to drink on a
Saturday night so close to a Sunday and especially not
in a cemetery.

Now in the twenty-first century, under the shifting
summer leaves of the perennials in the cemetery of this
presbyterian town, the Victorian and Edwardian angels
have been pockmarked with pellet dents. Some have
wings snapped in half or broken right off; bits of stone
wing litter the grass. There are spent cartridges by the
decorous peeping naked toes of one, more cartridges in
the grass by the stone plinth on which another sits, a
chalice in her hands and her nose shot away. The
occasional angel has been hit right in the eye or in the
middle of the forehead.

Lucky for the company that it was Kimberley
McKinlay who was the duty manager on the night shift

tonight when they came into the place wearing the hats over their faces with the eyeholes cut in them. It has all been recorded on the closed-circuit; the one at the front has the shears, the one in the middle has the saw, the one behind him has the leafblower kind of thing with the flex and the plug, you can see it trailing, and even more clearly you can see it jerking about in the air later when he waves the stick part of it at Rod who's on security tonight, though God knows what else he thought he was going to be doing with it, a leafblower for God's sake. But it is definitely threatening behaviour, especially the one with the shears, who came right up to the counter and jumped over it and threatened Michael Cardie who was on customer serving and pinned him to the wall, the blades open at his neck like a pair of scissors.

Would you like fries with that? is what Michael Cardie actually said to him, probably out of nerves, when he was pinned to the wall. Michael Cardie was pale and shaking afterwards. Kimberley sent him home early. She thinks he will be going up to the hospital getting treatment for shock for weeks to come after tonight. Kimberley herself will maybe get a medal. An OBE. A BCG. A BBC Digital. But no, because one day she really will be on the lists at New Year for her services to mankind, maybe when she's sixty, with her picture in the Highland News and everybody knowing because it will tell them in the paper how years ago, before she was the person she is going to become in her life, when she worked as the duty manager at the burger place at Tesco Village, there was absolutely no spitting allowed on the platelets of the flamegriller when it was her shift, absolutely none of that wanking into the mayonnaise bucket, and if it had been useless Kenny Paton who was on tonight it would all've been a different story, and apart from that, apart from tonight, honestly you really don't want to be eating anything from there the nights he's manager and all those boys sitting around on night shift bored out of their heads because Kenny Paton thinks the world owes him a living and never gets anyone to do anything properly.

In fact Kimberley McKinlay makes a point of dumping the old mayonnaise bucket no matter who's been on the shift before her, regardless of whether it's Kenny Paton or not. It is not real mayonnaise. It has some of the things in it that are in mayonnaise plus some preservatives and a sugar substitute. It tubes and spreads more easily than actual mayonnaise does. It doesn't stick to the equipment. It cleans off more easily. She begins every shift the same way; it is a ritual; she dumps the old bucket outside with the day's grease vats and takes the lid off a new bucket out of the stores. That way she can be absolutely sure. She has thought before now of reporting Kenny Paton, but she would never grass so it won't be her who reports it. The duty manager from hell. She won't be it. He's it. The nights he's on and someone feels peckish at half-past one in the morning they should leave the car in the garage and stay at home and if they're hungry eat some toast; there

should be a phoneline they can call to let them know
whether it's him who's on so they'd know not to bother
coming out the bloody road all the way to Tesco
Village just to eat wank and not know it, that's what
Kimberley thinks on her way home at half-past seven in
the morning, blinking in her car at the bright light of
day after a night of the fluorescent light at work, you
never know what it's like outside since there's no
windows. It could be raining or snowing or sheep and
pigs could be falling out of the sky, you'd never know
till you came out of work and found your car covered
in them, and it's a beautiful summer morning today,
the car starts easily when she turns the key, it's going to
be hot later, it's going to be a real beauty and she'll be
asleep all through it aye well that's life and work for
you isn't it.

The pay is £420 a week before tax, for managers,
with increments. It's not a hard job. Not many people
want to eat fast food in the middle of the night though
Kimberley can imagine it's different in the south where
there are more people who are stupider about what
they do with their time and money and digestive
systems. She knows she wouldn't want to. You get the
occasional mad person, but not that many mad people
have cars, thank God, or are bothered to walk out as
far as Tesco Village. You get sad persons and lonely
persons. You have to know how to deal with it. You
have to keep the druggies out of the toilets in the winter
but in the summer there are a lot less of them. You get
drunks, loud fourteen-year-olds who should be in their

beds, you get couples either snogging or arguing and
the call-girls meeting the men who they make money
off in the Tesco car park. You get homosexuals that
have nowhere else to go. Kimberley is always throwing
them out. You get bored taxi drivers. She might marry
a taxi driver one day, you'd get peace from each other
with a man with a job like that. You get people from
the supermarket on the three nights it stays open. Very
occasionally you get a family with kids at four in the
morning wanting all the breakfast items. But usually
it's dead. There's an after-cinema rush from the multi-
screen, an after-pub rush of people who shouldn't be
driving, then the long dead stretch for hours.

Except that there's never nothing to do, there's
cleaning to do so get cleaning, because when Kimberley
first started here on the night shifts she went in circles
from the stores to the kitchen to the food area to the till
area out to the customer area then the wiping down of
the seating, especially the difficult dipped places in the
plastic where the food congeals on the seats that are
shaped like the monster's humps and head, she was
scraping it out of the monster's eyes and tail-spikes on
her first night; they are lucky to have those monster
seats, actually, since the burger places up and down
the country are usually not differentiated at all. The
manager then, whose name was Tony, who is running
something important at head office in London now,
noticed her initiative and how she did the display stuff
up at the ceiling level which is always covered in bits of
food and small dead insects and fluff and grit, it's

through the air-conditioning that it gets up there, she still likes to clean it, it is very satisfying and that's how she got promoted, she got his job, one of the first females to manage a night shift for the company, she is a test case, maybe she will get an even better job like him after this though there's no way anyone on the company's going to know about this, she's telling no one, and there's absolutely no way anyway that she'd move down there, no way on earth, it'd have to be an important job up here.

Leave him alone, Kimberley McKinlay roared at the one with the shears when she came flying out of the stores to see what was going on out the front, apparently she was roaring like a lion in a rage as she came, she can hardly remember, that boy Dallas told her later she was shouting how the blades were filthy and he'd to get them away from the food area, and if he harmed the paintwork there'd be her to answer to, and how he could be giving Michael Cardie tetanus if he cut him with rusty blades. Imagine herself like that, roaring like a lion. Kimberley remembers the lions at the circus at Bught Park when she was a child, going round swiping at each other with their paws in a see-through tube that ran round the ring by the feet of the audience. She drives the long straight route back into the town with both the visors down, shielding her eyes with her left hand and feeling the serious frown on her face; she is young, she is driving as fast as her car will go, she is ready for anything and she is a person capable of serious anger. She wonders, when cars come towards her and pass her and she can see the strangers in them for the moment it takes two cars to flash past each other on a road, so fast that all you catch is a glimpse of face, what the people in those cars would think if they knew, and there is a kind of a pleasure all the same in knowing that they never will.

In they came to rob the place and she apparently stood square in front of the tills with her arms folded (she can't remember that). They wanted the money. You're getting no takings from here, she said, all you'll get from here is something off the menu and you'll pay for it before you get it too, and I'm only telling you one more time, get those gardening things out of here, they could be covered in e.coli and there's no gardening tools allowed in this restaurant, if you're wanting anything to eat you'll have to leave them outside the door.

They had the woolly hats with eyeholes in them pulled over their faces so nobody would know who they were but when one of them heard her say that it made him laugh inside the wool like he couldn't help it, it was the one with the saw, and when his arm went down to his side she noticed his other arm, that it had a false hand on the end of it, a hand that wasn't real, that's when she recognized him, it was Jason Robertson from Kinmylies who lost his arm in that motorbike accident and he scarred up his face too, she knew him from five years ago from when they were at school, everybody knew who he was after that happened. Are you not Jason Robertson? she said, and the one with

80

the shears swore and the other one waiting at the door
with the leafblower threw the leafblower down and
said I told you to put your fucking jacket over it. So
one of these boys would be Rich Riach, since him and
Jason Robertson were always hanging about together,
and there was something familiar about the one with
the shears, she was right, it was him under that hat
with the holes in it, but she still has no idea who the
other one at the door was, they called him Kevin, or
maybe it was Gavin. Rich she remembers wasn't really
called Rich, really he was Gordon Riach from the
houses over the other side of the canal. He was good at
football back then. He was still holding Michael Cardie
against the wall with the shears with one hand; with
the other he had lifted half the hat over his face, up
above his nose, and was getting a cigarette out of a
packet with his mouth.

There's no smoking in here, you, Kimberley said.

Rich Riach dropped the cigarette out of his mouth
when he opened his mouth to swear at her. Then he
couldn't hold Michael Cardie against the wall and
reach the cigarette he'd dropped. Jason Robertson was
looking at Kimberley. She could see his eyes through
the holes in the wool.

I'm not Jason Robertson, he said.

I knew you at school, Kimberley said, and saw his
eyes check her name badge.

Kimberley McKinlay, he said.

I wasn't in your class, she said, you won't remember
me.

I'm not Jason Robertson, he said again.

Security's coming, Jase, the one they called Kevin or Gavin said.

Kimberley McKinlay raised her eyebrows. Jason Robertson rolled his eyes. Kevin or Gavin stood behind the door with the leafblower held above his head, as if to smash it down on whoever came in.

The security man's name is Rod, Kimberley said to Jason Robertson. He's in his late fifties. His wife doesn't keep well. And you're being recorded on the closed-circuit cameras.

Jason Robertson's eyes, deep in behind the roughly cut wool, were like if eyes had no face.

We taped over the car number plates with that brown parcel tape, he said. The back and the front. There's no way they could trace it, like.

What he meant was, if she didn't give it away to anyone, who they were.

Tell him to take his shears off the neck of my employee, Kimberley said. She looked straight back at the eyes. She didn't blink.

Imagine having a hand that isn't yours, a hand that isn't a hand. Imagine not having the hand you were born with. Kimberley, driving home now from work, watches her hand changing gear. It is such a natural thing to do with your hand, change gear. You do it without even really knowing you're doing it. Her hand is well-manicured. Nowadays it is a manager's hand. She turns it over, palm up, glances down at it then back at the road ahead. This is the part of herself she would have lost if she was him. She knows where her heart line and her head line and her lifeline are. The right is the hand of realization, what you actually do with your life, the left is the hand of potential, what you're served at birth, she knows from books. Imagine not having your lines, leaving them somewhere, like a fox or a rabbit leaving a paw in a trap. No, much worse than a trap. He will have come off the bike at speed and hit the ground or wherever it was he hit at a rate that lost him his arm there and then, maybe, not even feeling it because of the adrenalin, off to the hospital not even knowing. Or maybe it was burnt too badly and later they had to remove it. She doesn't know. She knows he was on a motorbike, and a car or something came round the corner and he swerved to avoid the car and he hit something on his bike and the bike went up in flames, and at the hospital they had to do surgery on his face. She can't remember what he looked like before. He was a boy at school with light-coloured hair. Afterwards he left school. She was once in a pub and he was there too, afterwards. She hadn't looked, and then when she got home and went to bed she was ashamed of herself in the dark, that she hadn't.

She indicates left though there's no one behind or ahead of her.

Then old Rod the security man came in. He stood in the middle of the room and stared at the boys in the hats with the holes in them as if he'd just woken up. He looked too old. The colours in the place always make him look it.

Kimberley assured him there was no trouble.

I saw something on the monitors, he said. He spoke only to Kimberley. What've they the things on their heads for? he said.

Kimberley shrugged. Don't ask me, she said.

Fashion statement, Jason Robertson said.

They're trying to sell me their old gardening junk, she said. They're just leaving. Michael's just getting them their order. Michael?

Michael's been sick on the floor, Dallas said.

Dallas, get the mop and clean that, Kimberley said. She stood behind the other till and rang her code-number in. The till lit up. Now, what was it you were wanting again, boys? she said, and all three of them turned and tilted their heads, still in the wool hats, up at the menu boards above her.

Kimberley, who is good at reversing, reverses neatly into a small space and turns the engine off. She sinks back in the seat. She looks at the front of the house where she lives. Her sisters are asleep inside it, one at the back of the house, one at the front. Those curtains could do with a wash; she will be sure to remember to do it tonight before she goes back to work. She rests her head on the steering wheel.

Sit down, she said to them after she took their order, I'll bring it over.

Rich Riach took the hat off his face at last and the other one took off his too, they were sweating and red-faced under them; bits of fluff were stuck in the creases round the other one's nose. She definitely didn't recognize him. It was funny to see Rich Riach again, looking that much older. She remembered him when she saw him. Jason Robertson left his on. He stayed up at the counter to help carry the stuff over. Rich is poor; Jason Robertson told her Rich is in debt and wanted the money to take his wife on holiday because she doesn't believe he loves her since she found out he had an affair with a barmaid at the Lochardil Hotel. The one called Kevin or Gavin is out of work, he used to work on the rig site; he wanted the money so he could pay for an operation to have his ears pinned back, he thinks they stick out too much and that this has ruined his life so far, though Kimberley took a look at him and couldn't see anything wrong with his ears, they maybe stuck out a bit, not that much. He looked really happy when Rod bought the leafblower off him for fifteen quid before he went back to security, though fifteen quid won't make much difference, Jason told her the operation will cost a fortune if he wants it private. Kimberley asked what Jason Robertson wanted. I don't want anything, he said, I hate the food here. Kimberley laughed. Do the closed-circuit cameras record things twenty-four seven? Jason Robertson asked her.

He told her they've got hold of the blueprints the company use for all their burger places and they're all the same, wherever you go in the country. Up at the counter he asked her to tell him where in the building they keep the safe, so that the next place they decide to do they'll know exactly where to go. In the store, she said, and pointed with her eyes.

What Kimberley McKinlay wants herself is a new car. She wants to not still be paying so much money every month for this useless car which only starts if the weather's dry and what use is that? She wants a holiday. She wants some time in the sun. She wants to be able to sleep when it's dark, for once. She wants to not have to know that there are bits of food going round and round in the air-conditioning. She wants the last four years back. She wants to be the one going to the college this September and studying media studies, whatever the hell they might be when they're at home. She wants to be twelve again and to not have to think about anything, to be twelve and be able to go into a burger place on a summer's day like today and order things and eat them at a table, and she wants someone to be up when she gets out of this car in a minute and goes into the house, and she wants someone to have made the bed she's about to get back into, the one which will still be exactly as it was when she got out of it yesterday afternoon. She wants the same things that everyone wants and over and above those she wants it known, without her having to do the embarrassing telling of it herself, that there's no spitting or wanking on her shift like there is on other people's shifts, that there's no messing with Kimberley McKinlay mark my words.

She took the money for the food they ate out of Rod's fifteen pounds and gave them back the change and they left. Then she sent Michael Cardie home in a taxi.

You were amazing, Dallas said. You came, like,

roaring out of nowhere, like a lion, he told her. You were shouting about get those filthy blades away from my food area, there's no gardening tools allowed in this restaurant, and if you chip my paintwork, and you could be giving Michael Cardie tetanus, and if you hurt any of my staff. Man, it was something to see.

And I'm telling you, Kimberley McKinlay roared last night on the graveyard shift like a lion in a rage out at the burger place at Tesco Village: listen to me, she roared. If you lay a finger on, if you even sneeze on, if you even so much as give a single member of my staff a single germ I mean it you loser I don't care who you are there'll be hell to pay.

She takes the key out of the ignition, opens the door and the heat of the sun is on her back already. She doesn't really know that boy Dallas; he is usually on Paton's shift. She likes him. He's a good worker. She will ask the head of division if she can have him moved to her shift and if she does the asking right she will maybe get her way.

All the way up the front path she keeps one hand behind her back and throws the car key into the air with the other, catching it single-handed as it comes down.

It is a beauty of a day and Gemma the Cruise Assistant is stuck down here for the whole turnaround hour of the longest sunniest day of the year guarding four boxes of crisps and half a shelf of whisky miniatures from two of the fuckers.

It is so hot today that the flooring beneath her feet is dry. It is never dry down here. It is never this hot. It is the kind of day it is possible to get sunstroke on, and she is missing it. It's true, the scenery will be amazing today. She is supposed to love it. She does. She wouldn't be Scottish if she didn't. She is supposed to be proud of it. She wouldn't be Scottish if she wasn't. They will be taking film of it. They wouldn't be fuckers if they didn't. They will be taking pictures of themselves standing in front of it. They maybe wouldn't know they were alive if they didn't, it would maybe mean they were dead, or lost, or somehow naked, if they weren't looking through a camera at where they were. They film the water in front of them hoping something'll come up out of it and they'll be the ones who have it on tape. They lean over the rails and they film the surface of the water as the boat cuts through it. They film any old rubbish. They film cars going along the loch road. They film the trees on either side of the loch. They love to film all the palaver of going through the locks. They always film the castle, it's a heritage site, and they film the boats from the other companies that go past full of other fuckers filming them back. There's always at least one fucker wanting to take film of her too, and a lot more than just the one on the days it's raining and they're all squashed in downstairs freezing cold with their cagoules zipped up and the boat moving making them feel sick, sitting there filming the rain on the windows and her standing like she is now behind the bar.

Today, though, almost the whole one hundred and thirty-nine capacity (two exceptions: the woman going on about how sore her head is in German and the foreign girl reading the book) spent the cruise up on the deck, except for when they were queueing down here. They came down sun-dazed into the dark, holding the walls to get their bearings, walking blindly into the benches screwed to the floor, squinting up at the bar list and down at the money in their hands, talking about what a beautiful day it is, and it is a beauty, she'd hung around up on deck for as long as possible after departure before Andy, *good morning ladies and gentlemen, I'm Andy, your skipper on the* Bonnie Prince, *welcome aboard for today's trip along the Caledonian Canal and into Loch Ness, one of the world's most beautiful water-*ways, famed beauty spots and home of the famous Nessie, yeah, right, skipper, and him not even able to swim for fuck sake and God knows what would happen in an emergency, sent her down to open up, but not before she'd got some sun at least and made a twenty quid tip into the bargain. You will need it for your studies, the lady said. She was an old lady; she was staring at the hills, she said her family was once from here; beautiful, she said in her accent and looked lost and hurt, and pressed the money really hard into her hand. Her husband held his Sony up. He was old too. Twenty pounds for being nice to two old people from Canada for a minute or two. She didn't want their money. But they wanted to, that's why she took it, and she always gives the fuckers what they want. It

is part of the job. It is like pedestrians having right of
way in the Highway Code. Anyway she is out of here
in three months' time and away. That's only twelve
weeks. She is out of here in less than that; ten and a
half weeks to be exact. It is not that long. It isn't hard
to be polite. They're on holiday. They don't care that
most of the photographs are faked, or that the most
famous one, of the neck and the head coming out of the
water, is a newspaper scam that fooled people for
decades.

*Course there is. Course I do. I wouldn't be Scottish if
I didn't.*

*No no, there's hundreds of local people've seen her
over the years. Hundreds of people in history too,
including saints, and why would a saint lie?*

*Well, she's very shy, but keep your eyes open and
you never know.*

*Well I haven't myself yet, but there's always today,
eh?*

*Aye, it's a very mysterious place, you never know
your luck.*

*Aye, of course you can, on you go. Is it running?
Okay? Welcome to the Highlands, and to the* Bonnie
Prince, *the chief Highland Cruises cruiser. This is Loch
Ness, the home of the monster, and it's Thursday the
twenty-first of June. Will that do? Gemma. McKinlay.
McKinlay. It is, actually; it's related to the Buchanans,
and apparently they're maybe the oldest, the first, clan
society in the whole of Scottish history. Uh huh, of
course, I think a kind of a yellowy red one, and there's*

blue and green in it too. I know! No, my holiday job.
College. Ha ha, well, you know, actually there is such a
thing, I'm not going to be studying it myself, like, but
there are people who study the loch all the time, and
you know apparently the loch floor, the soil down
there, like right at the very bottom, the deepest parts,
it's very deep, the loch, and the soil from it is really rich
with nematodes that they can't find a match for anywhere else in the world or in the history of nematodes.
Nematodes. Eh, I don't know how. En ee em eh tee oh
dee ee es? I think. Ha ha, probably! That'll be right! All
the best! Eh, Gemma. Gee ee double em eh. Like Emma
but with a G. No, no, don't be daft, I'm not needing
any –. Aw. Are you sure? Well, thank you, it's really
awful nice of you. Thanks again. Och no. Have a good
holiday. See you later. All the best.

Of course there is. No question. It's a very
mysterious place. People, scientists, have actually seen
things on echo-sounders that they can't identify or
anything. Uh huh, down the stairs on the lower deck, a
range of hot snacks, light refreshments and we also
have a licensed bar.

Well I haven't myself yet. But there's always today,
eh?

Course I do. Course there is. Well, I haven't myself,
but I know she's there, and you never know, today
might be the day, it's a beautiful day for it, eh?

Beautiful. She is stuck on the boat for another four
hours, stuck behind here till they all get back on the
boat, free admission to the castle included on their

cruise ticket then Highland Cruises charge the stupid fuckers another fifteen quid for a ticket back on the boat again if they don't want to take the bus, and there's going to be nothing but complaining all the way home about how there's no soft drinks and how it's lunchtime and there's only crisps left, and she will be stuck behind here taking the complaints all the way back to the canal bridge.

The German woman is on her back with her eyes closed on the bench. Gemma knows she is German because she was speaking German when she came down the stairs holding her head, and her Loch Ness leaflet, on the floor, Gemma will have to pick it up later with all the other stuff that gets dropped on the floor, is in German. The girl reading the book by the door is something else, Gemma doesn't know what, her clothes look expensive, she is pretty, handsome almost, dark and continental-looking, from somewhere else, some-where that's always warm, and she is not the least bit interested in the loch or the trees or the castle or the monster or any of it, she's been down here by herself reading that book since the boat left. She looks like she's reading it backwards. She looks about the same age as Gemma. Why would you go on a cruise of Loch Ness, why would you buy a ticket for it, if you didn't want to see the things you were supposed to see on the cruise? That girl is not in the least interested in the fact that she's free to choose to read a book in the dark on the sunniest day there has ever been in the whole of Highland history while other people are stuck down here for four more hours of missed perfect sun and the Cokes practically all gone as early as Dochgarroch this morning and the mineral waters sold out, and fuckers really like to buy water, and the hot snacks finished and she's very low on spirits.

But in ten and a half weeks' time she will be studying *what images mean and how they mean in contemporary culture* as it says in the prospectus. She will be living in a big city she has only been to twice before. Nobody will know who she is. Nobody will care what she does. She will not be anywhere near this beautiful (she wouldn't be Scottish if she didn't) place she is so proud of, nowhere near this boat, the boring beautiful trees, the endless queues of people from other places all looking at the boring beautiful water. She will not have anyone telling her when she's allowed in the sun and when she isn't, or anyone breathing down her neck every time she goes into the stock cupboard at the office, pushing in behind her looking for what he can get then when he doesn't get it watching her like he's making sure she's not taking anything out of there that's not hers, reminding her who owns the boat, who's paying her wages, and on a beauty of a day like it is today she will be free to go home after classes, or whatever it is the shape of the days in the new place will be, and there'll be nothing on her back, nobody else she has to be watching out for or worried about. The lady over the road whose niece teaches at the school stopped her in the street and told her, on the quiet on her way home from work yesterday, that

Jasmine is telling people at the school, and not just any old people but her guidance teacher, that their parents drowned, it was in a speedboat accident apparently. When she got home last night Jasmine was out. She was still out after midnight, and this morning Kimberley was asleep. In ten and a half weeks Kimberley will have to be the one who worries about twelve-year-olds being out after midnight and wherever the hell they are, because she herself will be somewhere else, elsewhere, far from here, finding out what images mean and why they are important.

Imagine if, after all, they actually were in a speedboat that overturned and threw the both of them flailing across a stretch of water, and down they went into the dark of it. That would be almost nice. It is quite inspired of Jasmine really. At least you would know where they were. At least you could look at the surface of the water and know that this was where they'd gone down. At least they would be dead and it would mean something, instead of just living somewhere else with other people they're having sex with. She imagines them in their best clothes, light holiday clothes, and they have a camera, like every other fucker, and they're filming the future come speeding towards them from behind what seems the safety of the windshield of the speedboat, and the nose of the boat is up as it cuts the loch, and it's the moment before it curves too fast and the front rises and rises in the air until it flips itself over like an omelette, or a pancake, which is something she remembers her mother making one time when they came home from school, on the Tuesday in spring you are supposed to have the pancakes on. She imagines the two of them standing awkwardly together like in the old wedding photographs, just standing with each other in the same space, and now their clothes are dated, but even so, it doesn't matter, and even a fast-moving engine-vibrating doomed petrol-explosion of a space, a space that is any second about to overturn, is a good option. Then both of them are shooting through the air, their arms and legs waving about, his silver-ribbed watch glinting as it flashes past on his hairy wrist, her sudden panic about what will happen to her hair when she hits the water, then if someone presses the button they can be paused like a freeze-frame on the video machine, held in air the moment before they disappear, and her and her sisters watching it not happen on the T V in the background as they sit round the table eating the pancakes with sugar on them and lemon, and a lemon was exotic, something they hardly ever had in the house, and Jasmine was only a tiny baby then and she herself was so small that the half-lemon, she remembers, was huge in her hand.

In her head she hears a voice saying something about the water.

She blinks. I'm sorry, I was miles away, she says.

The girl who was reading the book is standing in front of her at the bar.

On another planet, Gemma says. Can I help you?

Some water, the girl says. For that lady. I think she should maybe drink something.

I'm sorry, Gemma the Cruise Assistant says. We're completely sold out. I can make you a hot drink if you'd like to choose one from the Drinks List.

The girl frowns, smiles, shakes her head.

I don't want to buy water, she says, I just need you to give me some for the lady over there who's feeling unwell.

I'm sorry, Gemma the Cruise Assistant says. It's not allowed to just give out water. You have to buy bottled water, and I'm awful sorry but there's none left. If you could choose something else off the List.

She indicates the Drinks List framed on the wall next to the bar.

You're not allowed to give out water? the girl says. She looks Gemma the Cruise Assistant in the eye.

The boat shifts slightly beneath them.

That's right, Gemma says.

See that lady over there on the seat? the girl says. She's seriously dehydrated. She needs to drink something. Have you not got ordinary tap water? You must have. What do you use to make the coffee and tea?

The girl doesn't sound at all foreign, she actually sounds Scottish. But she doesn't look Scottish and the book in her hand on the bar is in a language with letters Gemma doesn't recognize; the language, whatever it is with its tailed and coily letters, makes her feel queasy, like she felt when she went to the Baptist church on Castle Street with her friend once, years ago, and the people in the congregation kept standing up and shouting stuff out about God whenever they felt like it, like mad people.

The girl is speaking slowly and clearly now as if she thinks Gemma is an idiot. The fucker.

I'm really sorry, madam, Gemma says. I'm not allowed to use the water for ordinary drinking, it's only to be used for hot drinks.

Why can't it be used for ordinary drinking? the girl says.

Anyway, the bar is closed, Gemma says.

The girl looks at Gemma as if she hasn't heard properly what she said. The bar is what? she says.

The bar has to close for the hour while the boat is empty, Gemma says. It's mandatory.

The girl snorts.

It's for licensing laws, Gemma says.

You just said I could buy something off the Drinks List, the girl says. Were you open then, ten seconds ago, and now you're shut?

I'm awful sorry, Gemma says.

The girl leans forward, still looking her square in the eyes. Her skin is definitely dark this close up though she still sounds really Glasgow. Gemma takes a step back.

Listen, you, the girl says. Do you know what dehydration actually does to someone?

While she is talking about blood and dizziness and seizures and hospitals, Gemma looks her back in the eye, maintains her polite face and thinks the word over and over in her head. Fucker fucker fucker fucker fucker. What are they like, the fuckers, coming here

and thinking just because they've bought their ticket
they can be telling people what to do? Coming here and
then not even wanting to see how beautiful the sights
are. Not even interested. Reading a book in a weirdo
language instead. Thinking the world owes them a
living. Gemma almost smirks, manages not to, nods
politely as if she's listening. When the girl has finished,
she smiles her most friendly smile at her, reaches up
above her head, pulls down the metal blind that shuts
the bar off from the rest of the room and locks it in
place with the padlock.

She can hear the girl's disbelief on the other side of
the blind. She jumps when the blind rattles, when the
girl hits at it a couple of times. She is full of sudden
excited glee; it is like a different person is in her, pushing against her own skin to get out of her. She puts her
arms around herself. Her heart is beating like mad. The
foreign girl can complain if she likes. She is out of here
in ten weeks and away.

The floor is covered in the ripped-up cardboard and
discarded plastic of a busy morning. The rubbish bin is
overflowing at the back. Whose idea was it to call them
fuckers? She doesn't know; it is what everyone calls
them on the boat and in the boat office. Every morning
the queue of them waiting to get on the boat reaches
all the way to the main road. They wear bright colours
and sunglasses, they carry all manner of useless stuff
around with them. They're so hopeful, like dogs
waiting for their time for a walk.

There isn't much light in here with the blind down.

The only window is small and blocked by the fridge; through the crack of daylight visible she can see the castle outside falling and lifting. There isn't much room to move, and there is nothing left to drink except the coffee and tea water, and she can't drink that, she'll need it all the way back.

That German woman might die.

She wonders what the girl is doing. If it was her out there, and it was an emergency, she'd go round the boat collecting the dregs from other people's glasses and cans and bottles and give her that. She wonders if that's what that girl is doing now. She puts her head close to the blind but she can't hear anything. The astonishing thing about that girl is how smooth her skin was. When she brought her face close to Gemma's across the bar Gemma had seen its surface, and how her eyes were, they were

She sinks on to the bar stool. The eyes were beautiful. The beautifulness of them has sliced so deep into her without her even knowing that's what it was doing that she stares at the blind straight ahead of her because if she looks down she might see herself peeled back, opened at the skin; she doesn't dare look down in case she is actually bleeding. She remembers the wounded look on the face of the old Canadian lady as she stood on the deck and stared out at the summer land. She fingers the twenty pound note in her pocket. Somewhere in Canada in the future she will be smiling off a screen, telling people she's never seen and never will things about tartan and clans and the place she's from. Her voice will come out of a TV into the air of a place she has no idea about. There are versions of her all over the world by now; smiling versions of her have crossed so many seas and she doesn't even know it.

Maybe she should push the blind up and go out there and help the girl. She should use the hot drinks water. Nobody will know; she will say they sold a huge number of teas and coffees. It's such a hot day. Nobody will wonder. She will put in money out of her pay to make it look like more were sold. She will hide a pile of sachets and tea bags in her rucksack. The German woman will blink and nod and say she saved her life. The girl with the eyes that can read unexpected languages will smile at her. Maybe she is from the city that Gemma is going to be studying in. Maybe when the boat docks today and Gemma leaves for home, the girl will tuck the book under her arm and follow Gemma the Cruise Assistant home at a distance, being shy, and knowing Gemma is shy. On the way home Gemma will slow down and let her catch up; they will walk past the cemetery along to the end of the canal and down into the town, and Gemma will show her the sights. The art gallery. The museum. The cathedral. The theatre. The castle. The rabbits eating the grass on the hill under the castle, if they are patient enough to catch sight of them. The seals in the river, if they're lucky, if the river is low. The places where Gemma went to school. The boat office. Gemma has a key; everybody else will have gone home. There will be nobody else in there, it will be empty, and the light will be evening light by then. She tosses her hair. She takes a deep breath.

When she reaches to open the blind she finds it's locked. Then she can't find the tiny key she needs for the padlock anywhere. She looks on all the surfaces. She goes through all her pockets one by one, then does this over again. She looks all around her on the floor. She empties the rubbish out and checks through it. She picks up the stool. She empties the sachet boxes. She looks behind the whisky miniatures.

She pulls at the padlock but though it's only a small one it won't give. She turns it up the way so she can see its slot. She pokes at it with her nail, then lets it drop. She can't remember whether Andy has a key for it or not. She sits back down on the stool.

There is nothing to do about it. The room she is in sways because the boat is swaying on the surface of the water, tugging at the ropes that hold it to the dock, and it is nowhere even near time to go yet, so nobody will find her for ages, and it is hot, it is almost airless, and now she is thirsty herself and there is absolutely nothing in here that she is allowed to drink.

She is drunk it is theee ooonly waay to beee. The trees have moveen tops look. It is good drunk. It is better than good, it is the only way, drunk as a skunk is it ck? as a sck un ck drun ck and even though she is it, even though she is out of her brain like, she is pretty good becaaaause she can still. Really straight like a marksman man, like a expert marksman man, really. She hit it she must have like really good aim to be so pissed and still hit it. She heard it hit the stone IN LOVING MEMORY CHARLES ROBERT CAMERON BORN 4 DECEMBER 1907 DIED 18 MARCH 1978 THE LORD GAVETH AND THE LORD TAKETH AWAY bottle never broke kind of, uh. Bounced, uh huh, must have hit it on the thick glass bit of it not the thin glass bit of it. So she can throw it again if she gets up and goes over and gets it back, she can throw it again if she gets up and. She is smashed, not it. Ha ha ha. She is the thin. She is what is it out of her brain is what she is, out of her b.

Never even broke rememer don't forget it it is a good thing to. She has drunk it all now it is all finished because the other two bottles are broken on the gr gl ass. The bonnie g l r ass of Inverness, poem at school, Culloden the massacre and the Jacobites and the girl after and a tragedy, when all Jacobites were massacred and the girl is made like really sad because of it. Bonnie ass of Inver no bony ass of hee hee hee oho hohee hee hee hee. Bony oh ho hoo. Hoo. Other two broke on the stone when they were thrown. One second they were not broken they were bottles, and now. What can happen in a second, that, eh? cept not always, it doesn't always happen because look at that one it never broke when she threw, like, that is just amazeen. So there is it, that bottle still, should keep it for if he comes with the broken guns, in case, he might let her take a shot if he, because her good aim, she has aim, she has. What is just amazeen, just amazeen, is that it never. All them others are in pieces. The bottles labels paper holdeen

together broken bits BACARDI BREEZE. She had better
pick up the g l ass in case someone with a dog and the
dog's paws, it would be a shame for it. Lot of people
take their dogs for their walks in here but there is never
any dogshit she has seen, people are respectabful,
because of the dead like probly. She would like a dog.
She would keep it off the g r ass out of respect for them
on the underneath of it, them dead for years, they
wouldn't be wanteen to be walked on by paws of a dog
or peoples feet crosseen over their bodies and their
heads all day and ha! sometimes night too. Cathy
Maclennan at school shaggeen that Vaughn MacDonald
from third year up by the old graves and came down
the path half-past ten straighteneen her clothes and saw
her here on her way out from the shag, she had g r ass
stains, she was telleen him she left her mobile phone up
there, she said would he go and get it and he said no
way, you go, and she said, no way am I goeen back up
there it's near dark like, they were both goeen to each
other no, no way, then she seen her and goes look
theres that Jasmine McKinlay, so she shouts over to
Cathy Maclennan I don't mind goeen, whats your
mobile number and I could ring it on mine and then
you could hear it and find it, but Cathy Maclennan just
ignored her, like, as if she wasn even there, and says to
her next day at Home economics, they were doeen fruit
and cheese scones, she comes over and says I saw you
in the cemetery by yoursel you are fuckeen mental man,
there are druggies there and everytheen, you are mad
like always goeen in there by your sel I saw you

hangeen about, full o dead people, you're a weirdo to go there if youre not actually like shaggeen someone, huh, Cathy Maclennan is the bony ass of, just shoween off that she's got a shag, horrible fuckeen place, disgusteen morbud place Cathy Maclennan says to her, but then she said back to Cathy Maclennan, she said, well right when you like die will you be wanteen to go to heaven and Cathy Maclennan said well duh obviously, if there is one, and then *she* said, *she* said, well there you go because if its heaven then somebody must be dead, thats what heaven is int it, you cant get into it unless youre like out of it, ha ha ha, they had a notice up sayeen it wan a prize, it is actually the most the best-kept cemetery in the whole of SCOtland, probly because the g rass is always really neat and everytheen and when she comes back theyve always like cleared up the bottles she broke the last time she was here, doesn seem to matter where in the place she was breakeen them they find it and its gone, and there is never no noise except that birds, and the noises trees makes, and she has been here loads and never seen a druggy, not even one time, maybe if she sees one they could give her sometheen that would last longer than three fuckeen alcopops. Maybe if you are a druggy you might not want to be near a place like it, maybe you would halogenate, see the dead and everytheen. Except thon man, he isn't, because she said are you a druggy? and he says no. One was a air rifle, one is sometheen else, she has forgot remember och come on Jas remember, it is, ach, it is called a, cant, more power than the air rifle,

can blow off a hand or a big bit of the shoulder, she
watched and the whole shoulder, the whole of the
shoulder, was like just blown away to notheen, wee
flakes of stone, you never seen anytheen like it. He says
he knows her parents the man. If maybe he came
tonight and she has thon bottle she never broke, she
could ask. She could prop it on the top like and then if
he would let her take the gun because her aim, right?
Even when she is like even stocious as this, man. She hit
it for definite, its not that she missed it, it for definite
hit it, the stone, it just never broke. It is a mirage, like
when he made the wine out of notheen for them at the
weddeen in Religious Studies. It is a mirage that it
never broke. She could prop it on the head ha ha ha an
angel with it on its ha ha ha head. Hee hee hee hee hee.
Would you like a drink Mrs Angel, if it was red bull it
would give you wings ha ha ha you arent needeen them
you already got them look on your back, you been
drinkeen already hee hee hee an angel drinkeen a
Bacardi breezer hee in the clouds hee hee oh god feeleen
really oh feeleen sick now shit shit stop, right, sit for a
minute, there, sit still, there. There. There. Aye wait
though. Aye.

It is empty but it is no actually broken. A great noise
it makes though, though, it is a great noise. She really
really loves it, the sound of it when it breaks. Every
noise has its own noise of its own breakeen. When you
drop it froma bove its different the noise. When you
throw it really hard its different. When you drop it
gently the noise is more gentle. When you try not to

break it and it still breaks, that is a different noise again. They are all different and unique like every snowdrop that like falls from the sky above is, they are all formed from water crystals and no one is ever the same as any other one is, that is amazeen. Snow for fucks ake! There will never evr be snow again, it is so hot, God, it was the hottest day she can ever remember, it is not possible to have snow in her head even in her imanation, how could there ever be it, snow? Eh? Again? How? Eh? It is so warm in the world there will never be snow or Xmas or that again. Little do-nkey, carry Ma-ry safely on her wa-y. Ring out those bells tonight Bethlee eehem, Bethlee eehem, Ring out those hmm tonight the ground isn even dampish, summer is fuckeen fantastic like, she could sleep here tonight, it would be fine no body would come, they are lockeen the gates around tennish these nights, but it is still not dark or anytheen till after and they open it in the morneen for visitors to come first thing before their work she supposes to see their nearest and deadest, ha ha, in the morneen for the mourneen ha ha ha ha ha, last night it was morneen at like God knows she doesn't know really really early when she was walkeen home like, she never left here till it was like getteen light again and all and by the time she was home it was light.

What if Cathy Maclennan's mobile if it began to ring by itself up there and nobody answereen it, somebody at the other end listeneen to the ringeen, the beep of it somewhere in the grass, notheen but birds and trees and stones to hear it.

She wonders what tone it has. Is it a TV programme? or a S Club song. Or maybe it is switched off.

Fuck she is sobereen up, is she? Is she? Look at the, trees are still moveen their tops, it is near dark now but she knows it wont get much more it, but theres notheen left in any of these bottles whether theyre broken or no. She runs her fingr through where the label is holdeen the broken bits but theres notheen left to drink on the inside of the bits and no, careful or she cd, ah you bastard, ah, shit. She sucks it to stop it bleedeen. Thank god she never used her tongue to look for anytheen left. It is a pity there is none left since it is antispeptic. She will be a doctor and fix it all when she is qualified doing the qualifications at the college, they are sayeen at thon careers she could if she wants be whatever she wants because they are sayeen she is really like, you know, if she uses her brain, but they keep sayeen *you will have to want to nobody's goeen to do it for you except you* well but if you are and people see, like that girl Jacqui who no body will talk to because she is like so fuckeen swot, fuckeen thinks the world owes her a liveen like, look at her, and if you are it then you get all the time people goeen on about fuckeen who do you think you, all that stuff. No, it would be good to win the lottery like, you would never have to work, or famous on the TV, in a house like big brother or in a pop group that wins a TV phone-in with millions, or no, no because she will be a marksman, join the, whatever it is they need marksman for, must be loads they need them for. They must need people with aim.

Because even when she is skuncked, no skun k ed, shit,
it is beginning to come back, it is, och, beginning to,
shit. Is it? Is it? She bangs the back of her hand against
the trunk of the tree above her head, it is a pine tree,
och uh huh, not faraway enough the sore rough when
she hits it, och, fuck sake three isn't long enough, three,
it isn't even proprly night yet, look, still see them
moveen in the sky, and she is beginning to again. Finger
still bleedeen and its fuckeen sore. Three is not enough,
remember, next time Jas get four, maybe five, ask
Gemma for the money, say it is for a school trip to
Kincraig Wildlife Park. Maybe he will come again, that
was good last night when he did. It was nearly this
dark when he came. She could still see the tops of the
trees but only just. That would be good. If he was to
come again tonight. Last night she saw him, he was up
by the angels and she went over and asked him, he
jamp in the air when he saw her, she thought he was
maybe a druggy and wondered if he had anytheen, she
says to him, was he and he said no. He just stood and
looked at her and says it:

No.

What are you then, a gamekeeper then? she said. She
was quite sobery, she thought maybe it was for foxes or
birds or rats or whatever wasn't allowed in there that
he had the two guns, one on each arm, and they were
broken. The word you call them when theyre like
broken open, like at the place you load them they are
open, broken, on his arm, hanging over his arms one

each, good thing to remember, that, different thing broken can mean.

No.

Is it to shoot animals for fun, like?

No.

Is it to shoot at seagulls?

No.

Is it to shoot the trespassers, like druggies or that? are you a gatekeeper?

No.

Well if it's no to shoot anybody or anytheen that's liveen and there's notheen else in the place except dead people who aren't needeen shot, then what the fuck are you goeen to shoot at? she says. He looked kind of old, doesn't look like the kind that would be in a gang. He didn't look like the police or anytheen. He put one of the guns down and his foot on it.

Don't swear, he says.

He clicked the other together and put it up to his eye and shot it and the great noise it made and when it hit the angel the puff of stone off it, she went to look and it had hit it in the hand where the hand was held kind of draped over the heart, and the hand all cracked like its fingers dented by the pellets.

Fuckeen brilliant! she says, wiping the new-chip dust of the stone on her sweatshirt.

Come away from there, the man said whispereen, he waved her with his gun over towards him. Then he put down the gun and stood on it and picked up the other gun and clunked it together and looked down it and fired it at the angel. Its whole shoulder was gone. He was waiteen listeneen for the birds to stop makeen a noise and settle in the tree tops and then when they stopped he fired the same gun again and off they went squawkeen again. The top of the head and face blown away. Then he broke his guns open and hung them on his arms and turned and went.

Can I get a shot? she said.

Go away home to your bed girl, he says walkeen past her, you shouldna be out this late by yourself. Your parents are heathen to be letteen you.

She was like amazed. How do you know my parents? she called after his back.

The man stopped. He kind of like barked. He turned himself and his guns round and came back towards her. He stopped up next to one of the statues.

If you tell a soul you seen me, he says, God will punish you. So don't.

Okay, she says, she was thinkeen he can be a lame-o weirdo Godfreak if he wants. I wont tell if I can get a shot of your gun, she says.

The man looked at her as if measureen her for clothes. He looked at his watch. Then he looked up at the sky in the trees. He kind of breathed out. Quick, he said, before the light's back and anyone catches us.

He clunked the gun straight. Dont touch, he said. He held it to her eye. She looked down it and couldnt see anytheen, then the man put his hand on her head and made it hold still and she saw in a glass circle in the gun's telescope, swirling dark-light, it must have been the sky, then the trees close up, and the fence at the back by the canal then the gravestones like all wavereen about. Then he took the gun back.

Watch, the man said, and he held it to his head and shot it at the one with its hand fixed by its fingers to its chin. She went and ran and got the bit of stone off the grass. Some fingers were still stickeen out by themselves into the air off the chin, but the place there should be a hand they were attached to was empty. The hand was in bits on the grass. She brought a bit back. The man took it from her and threw it away into the bushes.

Now, he says, that one, and even though he was a bit old lookeen for it he went round on his heel like a cowboy in a film and shot the one in the head and the other in the Bible.

He is a minister in a church. The angels are idles. It is his job. He showed her the difference when a gun is ready and when it isn't.

Then the light came up properly and the man was off.

The colour of the stone inside the broken head of the one he shot the head and shoulder off was pure white when she looked. Tonight she looked again, all its wavy hair is down its other shoulder with no head left to grow out of. The man is a pure marksman so he is. He is a crackshot. Loads are damaged or decapitated in the bit of the cemetery where the angels are. There is only one bit of the cemetery that has angels, round by the canal, there aren't any angels anywhere else in it. It

is sometheen to do with one of the religions haveen
angels and one with none allowed.

 She is still wondereen how he knows her parents,
that man. They are notheen to do with religion. He
never answered her about it. Maybe he was haveen her
on. She is wondereen, if he does know them, like does
he know them both, or her mother or her father by
themselves. She wonders would he, like, say to them he
saw her and where she was and what time of night it
was and her out and not at home or anytheen. But as
long as he doesn't tell Kimberley it will be ok. She
wonders if he knows Kimberley. She is sober now. As
a, what is it that is supposed to be sober? Anyway she
can feel everyfuckeentheen, every thing there is in the
whole universe, she can feel it all. Wee scratchy stone
under her leg, tickly grass on her wrist, warm-cold off
the air all round her, sad off the lights that are on in all
the people's bedrooms in the houses over the canal that
she can see through the trees and the wire fence, and
her finger is still really stingeen and all. She has
wrapped a dock leaf round it and if she keeps holdeen
it tight it will not bleed.

 It is as dark as it is goeen to get, so if that man is
comeen he will be here any minute. She has the bottle
that never broke – it is amazeen that it didn't – but she
isnt drunk any more, not really, and really what she
was wanteen was to see if she could still hit it like when
she was completely out of it because that would be
really impressive. But it will still be good to see what
her aim is like when she isnt out of it too. Because first

she wants to know like, does she have aim. The gun was heavy-lookeen, the bigger one of them, and second is, will it be too hard for her to unbreak it, will someone need to help, or could she like do it hersel, is what she needs to know.

The angels are raising their eyes blank and seemly to the heavens.

The men are still carousing inside their hill of the dead.

The seagulls are gathering on the riverbank, ready for the morning.

Someone else is asleep in the locked concrete box, a girl-hitch-hiker with her head on her backpack maybe, or a tink they should chase, the police, never mind give him free room and board.

The thousands of rags on the trees at the old well weigh down the branches, unmoving.

The monster is deep in the bed of the loch, its big fin twitching, muddying the water with sediment.

The tourists are asleep in the hotels, the guest houses and the bed-and-breakfast beds.

The good people of the town. The bad people of the town.

In the middle of the night, light.

erosive

What do you need to know about me for this story? How old I am? how much I earn a year? what kind of car I drive? Look at me now, here I am at the beginning, the middle and the end all at once, in love with someone I can't have. The waking thought of her, sunlit and new, then the all-day hopeful lightheadedness, and behind it all, dull as a blown-out lightbulb, the fact of the word never.

I see someone in the mirror in the hall. I look again. It is me. It is the first time I have seen myself for days and I look as if I have been sleeping in my clothes. I go into the kitchen and I see how the piled-up dishes are coated in rot. I can't remember eating off any of them. I come through to the living room; the books are all over the floor.

I go out into the garden and I look at the apple tree. It is a new apple tree, I planted it three years ago. It is the same height as me. In its first year it gave one apple, edible, sharp-tasting and good. In its second it gave three. This year it is covered in small coming apples; there are more than ten. But its new leaves seem to be dying. When I look closer I see that the shoots on the branches are crowded with green and mauve aphids. The larger new leaves, the fronts of which look clear and clean, have insects packed like bricks on their undersides and the edges of several leaves have been rolled firmly in on themselves, which is killing them. When I uncurl them I find scenes of tiny grime, as if each rolled leaf holds inside it its own abandoned factory yard.

All around its base, going up and down the trunk of the young tree, balanced at the very ends of the branches, picking at the crammed-in aphids and the sweet tight newest possibilities of leaf: ants.

middle

Though I can't talk for long, my friend says, it's near London now and the tunnels start soon.

No, listen, I'm fine, I say. Really I am. Really good. Except that I wanted to ask you, there are these ants all over the apple tree and hundreds of greenfly on the leaves.

Don't put poison down, she says. You'll ruin the apples and the ground and the tree, never mind killing the ants. It's an ant farm. They'll be farming the greenfly. You'll have to ask them to leave. Be polite. Listen, I'm going into a

Monastery? Coma? Sulk? Whichever, her voice is gone. I hang up the phone and step over the books on the floor in the living room and go back out into the garden. I go straight to the tree and I find a branch with an ant probing its end. I lift the branch to my face until the ant is so close it has gone out of focus. It is unaware of me, of everything but the end of the branch which I hold to my mouth like a tannoy microphone. Please leave, I say. This is my apple tree and you're killing the leaves. Please tell the other ants to leave with you.

Doing some gardening? my neighbour asks across the fence.

What he really means and isn't saying is: why are you at home again in the middle of the afternoon and not at your work?

You're home early, I say.

Day off, he says. What about you? Not well?

What he means is: have you been made redundant? have you been fired? am I earning more than you now? will you still be able to afford the mortgage or will you have to sell your house? and how much will it be worth, because probably mine will be worth more since I've done more to improve mine than you have.

No no, I'm fine, I say. I tell him I'm on extended leave. Know anything about ants? I say.

Ants? he says. Got to kill them. It's the only way. Otherwise they spread all over.

What he means is: they'd better not spread into my garden.

He gets his mower out of his shed, mows his lawn

though he only mowed it three days ago, then puts his mower away again.

What he means is: you don't mow your lawn enough. Look at your garden. Look at it, for God's sake.

He goes indoors; I hear the slam of his back door. I have been waiting by the tree now for about half an hour. The ants don't seem to be doing anything different. They certainly don't seem to be leaving. I get the old bike out of the shed and I cycle it to the shopping complex and all the way there I am thinking about the skin on the underside of her arm and what it would feel like, and imagining the curve and weight of her breast as it rises over my mouth, past my eyes, so that when I get to the arcade I go into the supermarket because it's the shop I usually go into, rather than the DIY shop which is where I meant to go. I stand in the middle of the fruit and vegetable aisle and I have no idea why I'm here.

A trainee is stacking nectarines. She looks about fifteen. Her name badge says ANGELA HERE TO HELP.

I tell Angela about the ants. She looks at me as if she has never heard anything stranger in all her life. She looks at my clothes and at my hair. She backs away. After a few minutes a woman of about thirty comes towards me. Her badge says HELEN SELLAR SUPERVISOR.

Can I help you? she says.

I tell her about the ants.

Chilli powder, she says. An ant won't ever walk over

chilli powder. They don't like getting it on their legs.

Thank you, I say.

I go to the spice aisle and I buy four packets of mild chilli powder. I buy mild rather than strong because I am concerned not to hurt the ants too much. Angela and Helen Sellar watch me pay and watch me leave; they are still watching me as I unlock my bike from the window at the front of the shop.

When I get back to the garden I set up a border round the tree with the contents of two of the packets. The ants continue up and down and under the tree across the orange of the powder as if it isn't there, as if it's just so much more earth.

I go into the house and phone my father.

I'm watching the football, he says.

Don't hang up, I shout.

I call him straight back again. The phone rings for a long time.

What? he says when he picks it up. Well, you've got to paint your trunk of your tree white. They don't like white. They never cross white. Not the whole trunk, and not gloss for God's sake or you'll damage your tree. Emulsion. Put a ring of white around it, that'll stop them.

I go out to the shed again and I find an old tin of paint. I prise the lid off it with a screwdriver. I can't find a brush so I use the screwdriver to coat three inches of white all the way round near the base of the trunk.

I sit on the grass and wait for the paint to dry. I

watch to see that no ants will get stuck in it while it's wet.

end

I knock an ant off the end of a branch. I pick one off the tree and crush it. I see another running down the trunk and I kill it with my thumb. Several more ants panic on the trunk. I kill as many of them as possible. Then I stop killing them. They can kill the tree if they want. What can I do about it? Nothing.

I go indoors and start putting books back on the shelves alphabetically.

Later I go out into the garden again and dig round the tree. I dig right down to its roots. Even though this tree has only been here for three years its roots are very firm. I use the spade to slice through them and then with all my strength I lean backwards until I have pulled the tree out of the ground.

beginning

I fall in love.

More figuratively speaking, I am walking along the road one day when out of nowhere I am struck by lightning. The lightning is a freak accident; it is not raining, or even very cloudy, it is a fine day, though the weather has been very hot in the south and cooler in the north and presumably the lightning is something to do with the two fronts meeting. When they meet it is as if someone has hit me across the back of the head with a baseball bat or plugged me into a socket whose power lights up my whole body. I am dazed but I am glowing. I am so bright beneath my clothes that I have to shield my eyes. Light is streaming out of the ends of my sleeves over my hands. I put my hands under me and sit down blinking on the kerb.

She stops her car in the middle of the road. She leaves the door of it hanging open and comes over to where I'm sitting. She is lit, she is shining too. She looks like summer. I saw you, I saw it all, she tells me. She describes the sudden light darting out of the sky and tells me how it made direct contact with the back of my head. Sure enough, there is a burnt spot in my hair when I finger my skull and I can still smell the slight high scent of singe.

I can tell you her hair is yellow.

I can tell you she is around twenty-five.

I have no idea what kind of car it is she drives.

Days later, weeks later, possibly months, and I am in love with the sky, with the ground, with the bees cavorting in the pollen in the flowerheads. I wake up in love. I fall asleep in love. There are ants on my apple tree, killing its leaves. Let them. I love every single one of them, every single invisible DNA footprint they leave on its bark. Good luck to them. I hope their aphids thrive. I am in love with their aphids. I am in love, too, not just with my friend whom I love anyway because she is my friend, but also with my neighbour, and with Angela and Helen Sellar at the supermarket.

121

I am in love with my grouchy father. I come in from the garden and sit in my living room surrounded by books I have heaved off the shelves because otherwise will I ever pick them up and open them again? I open my old Chambers Twentieth Century Dictionary randomly. Everything is meaningful. Gordian: as in Gordian knot. Hylic means corporeal. Need means want of something which one cannot do without; a state that requires relief; necessity. Spelter is impure zinc. Gleam is a small stream of light, a beam, a brightness, often used figuratively itself, i.e., a gleam of hope, a gleam of understanding.

I lie on the floor with my head on my books and my feet up on more of my books and stare up at the ceiling with its flystuck old electric fitting and at this point in the story even the ceiling is glorious.

the book club

The girl who went missing was the same age as I was. Her school photograph was in the papers and on the Scottish news on television, which I found very exciting at the time since nothing about where we lived was ever on television, not even Scottish television. I was ten. I spent the long light nights that summer playing by myself in and out of the greenhouse my father was putting up in our back garden. It had no plants or glass in it yet, just the concrete floor, the frame of its sides and roof and the new door stiff in its runners. I could put my arm through glass that wasn't there and imagine it passing through solid wall, like in The Bionic Woman. I could lean out of the top half of the door like it was a stable door, or crouch down under the metal bar across its middle and walk through the bottom half of it without opening it.

I heard my father over the fence talking to someone by the garages. He called me out of our garden. She loves books, he was saying to the man. Here, he said to me, this man says he'll let you choose any book you like out of his van, then when you've read it you can give it back to him and get another one.

The man's name was Stephen; he sold books round the Highlands and Islands. The inside of his van was all books. It had folding steps at the back doors; it was all right to go in because my father had said it was. It wasn't a library, they weren't for borrowing, they were for selling. They had titles like Papillon and Shogun. I chose one about someone looking for someone, with the actress I now know to be Diane Keaton on the cover smiling and smoking a cigarette; I chose it because she was pretty.

If you're careful with it, the man from the van said, I'll be able to sell it on.

He showed me how to hold it and bend it gently so the spine wouldn't crease and so I wouldn't smear the page-edge with dirty hands. I read it in bed. It was about sex, then somebody killed her. Each night I held the book like he'd shown me because of the person who would be reading it after me, maybe someone who lived out on one of the islands. Someone up there would buy it from the van and would have it in their house and I had to make sure they would never know I had read it before them. There was a girl from the Outer Hebrides at my school. She spoke like her words had extra sounds to them, fussy-edged like the lace things my mother stuck with long pins on to the backs and arms of the new three-piece suite in the front room.

My mother, eyeing me blank and steady over the breakfast plates.

Iona, you're looking a bit pale, she said. Come here.

She felt my head. I had been awake long after everybody else, reading and re-reading the bits about sex and the part at the end where the man did it, holding the book as hardly open as possible with my head at an angle to try to make out the words at the hidden inside ends of the lines.

I was up late reading, I said.

She pushed the butter into her toast, hard and spare with the knife. Neither of my parents read books. If you worked you had no time for it. My mother especially had no time for it, she saw no point in it, which is why it's still surprising to me that one of the very few things I have of hers now, ten years after her death, is a book. Rip Van Winkle and other stories by Washington Irving. She gave it to me one afternoon when I was in my twenties, home from college for the summer; you can have this, she said. God knows where she'd kept it, I'd never seen it before and I knew every book in the house. It was a school book. It has her maiden name and the name of her school written in neat handwriting inside a printed shield saying This Book Belongs To, and her name scrawled in blotted blue capitals all along the page edge in messy different-sized letters. Its date of publication is 1938, the year her father died and she had to leave school. She was fourteen. Now I have the book, her grey leather driving gloves and her wedding ring.

I am thinking about all this between the airport and home, in a black cab crossing the South-East of England. The driver is keen to talk to me, I can sense it. I take a book out of my bag and hold it ready, though I know if I do actually try to read it I will get motion sickness. It's a book that was on a lot of shortlists last year. It's written by a man and the trick of it is that it's written as if a woman were writing it. Everybody says it's good. I turn it over in my hand. It smells of my father's tomatoes. I hold it to my nose and fan its pages. My bag is full of tomatoes, some near-ripe, some still green. I am supposed to put them on my windowsill when I get home.

The driver half turns towards me. I open the book in the middle. I glance at it, then out of the window. The grass on the road verges is high again, the fields the gold colour they go at this time of year. I press a button by my armrest and the glass to my right slides down. Summer air comes in. The summers go round and round, they seem not to get any older at all, they seem smooth, repetitive, summer back again, but really they date as hopelessly as if you put an old 45 on a turn-table, or maybe took an old 45 off a turntable and skimmed it into a canal on a still day like today then stood staring at the surface where there's nothing to say anything ever skimmed across it or sank below it or happened at all.

Now the driver is asking me something. Excuse me, he is saying from behind his divide. Where do you want?

His voice sounds amplified but far away. I've already told him where we're meant to be going. What if we're going the wrong way? I don't have that much cash on me and already the animated circle on his meter which lights a new piece of itself every three or four seconds and means ten pence each time the circle completes itself has completed itself an alarming number of times and we're only just on the outskirts of Luton.

I tell him the name of the town again.

No, but where? he says.

Near the centre, I'll tell you when we get there, I shout at the divide.

But where exactly? he says. The street you live in. How is it spelled?

You won't know it, I shout. It's very small.

You don't need to speak so loud, he says. I can hear you.

Without taking his eyes off the road he points to a sign above the back of his head. When the light is on, the sign says, you may speak to your driver.

Oh, right, I shout. Then I speak more normally. The street I live in is very small, I say, but when we get there I'll tell you which way to go.

No, he says. Because look.

He has a screen stuck to his dashboard about the size of a paperback. He flips its insides down and open. He punches some buttons.

I just told it the city we're going to, he says.

A voice comes out of the screen, the voice of a middle-class English lady. She says: *at the next roundabout, continue straight ahead.* Words appear on the screen at the same time saying the same thing.

We come to a roundabout. We continue straight ahead.

So where do you live exactly? the driver says.

He enters the name of my street into his machine. Several maps flash up. That's where you live, isn't it? is that where you live? he is saying. There? He swivels his head from me to the road ahead then back to me then to the road again. The cab swerves as he turns. I slide about on the seat.

Yes, I say.

See? he says. It's good, isn't it? It can tell you about anywhere. Anywhere you ask it. Anywhere at all. It sends a signal to the satellite and the satellite sends a signal back.

He points at a small dark box fitted on to the other side of his cab.

And you can have the voice on to tell you, or just the words on here if you don't want to listen to the voice, or both, if you want both, or neither, if you don't want a voice or the information, he says.

He switches the voice on and off to show me. He turns its volume up and down. He is a lot younger than me. It's a new cab. Everything metal about it is reflecting light and its grey insides are new. It says on a sticker by my hand on the door the words Made In Coventry With Pride.

It cost eighteen hundred, he says, and that's not all it does. It tells you, look, it tells you all these things.

At the next roundabout, the lady's voice says, *continue straight ahead*.

He presses a series of buttons one after another.

It tells me the fastest route, he says. And the route that is quietest. It tells me exactly how many miles till I have to turn left or right. It tells me about roadworks. It tells me how many miles it is to your house, not just to the city but right to your house. And look, it can tell me the route that saves me petrol, and when we get to town it will tell me exactly which way to go to get to your house and exactly how many yards before I have to turn left or right to get there. See that roadsign? What does it say?

Bedford 15 miles, I say.

Look on here, look, what does it say?

Bedford 15 miles, I say.

Exactly, he says. Exactly. So if we wanted to go to Bedford, we would know for certain without needing a roadsign that it's only fifteen miles away. Did you ever travel in a cab like this before?

No, I say, this is my first.

I wonder to myself if it is an elaborate chat-up technique. Do you want to go to Bedford. He tells me that soon all cabs and probably all cars will have navigation systems like his.

My name is Wasim, he says. I'll give you my mobile number and whenever you need a cab from Luton you can call me and I'll always fetch you from the airport.

What? he says when I tell him my name. How is it spelled?

He tries to make sense of it.

It sounds like three words, not one, he says.

It's the name of an island, I say. It's a place. You could type it into your machine and find me on it.

Ha ha, he says. But where are you from, if it is okay to ask?

I point to the screen. You know exactly, I say.

Ah, he says. No, before that. You're from somewhere else. I can tell by the way you speak.

At the next junction, the middle-class lady's voice says, *turn left*.

He tells me he has a cousin who works in Glasgow. I tell him Glasgow's not really near where I'm from.

I visited, he says. It rained.

He lifts both hands off the wheel in a shrug which takes in the whole country round us, deep in its afternoon sun.

I nod and smile. I sit back.

Are you too hot? Do you need air-conditioning? Tell me if you need anything, he says.

I'm fine, I say. Thank you.

If you want to go to sleep, go ahead, he says. I'll wake you when you're near home.

He flicks a switch on the dashboard. The little red light above his head goes out.

Her name was Carolyn Fergusson, she lived down the Ferry, it was before the new bridge and I can remember the posters stuck on the shop windows with her school photograph on them, she looked sad. They found her in her uncle's house up in Kinmylies hidden all over the place in supermarket bags in the cupboards, I remember a friend of my parents coming round to the house and telling them; he knew because he worked at the police labs, and that the smell when they went in was really terrible even though the summer hadn't been nearly as hot as the one the year before; they were in the kitchen talking about it and I was listening through the door and when they heard me there my mother shouted at me to go out to the back garden and bring the washing in. That summer I Feel Love by Donna Summer was number one for weeks and after it the Brotherhood of Man. Running away together, running away for ever, Angelo. Whenever I hear those songs now I think of then. We weren't supposed to leave our gardens; we were supposed to stay where our parents could see us at all times. The following summer we could go where we liked again and I can't remember what was number one.

Next to the tomatoes in the bag is the lump of defrosting soup in its Tupperware container; he wrapped it in newspaper to keep it cool. He is refusing to take any of the pills his doctor told him to take. He was proud about it. You're being stupid, I said. Rubbish, he said, they do you more harm than good. He took me out into his garden and pointed at some huge concrete slabs by the greenhouse and said, as soon as you've gone I'm going to take those seven slabs up and put them back down on the other side of the garden and then I can swing the caravan round on to them, and then there's a fridge-freezer in the garage I'm going to move into the house later today if I can get it through the door. You are joking, aren't you, I said. But he's a bit deaf in one ear and he was looking away from me with the wrong ear turned towards me, he didn't answer.

I feel the cab turn left. The soup is wrapped in newspaper covered with the story of the missing schoolgirls, which is why, I suppose, I'm even thinking of Carolyn Fergusson. It's pushed the build-up of war on to the second and third and international pages. It's always in the summer they go missing, as if it's the right season for it, as if the people who take them have been waiting, like farmers or fruit pickers or tabloid editors, for the right weather to kick in for it. When I was about twelve and got home late one summer night, when they'd been calling me and calling me all round the neighbourhood to come in and I hadn't heard, they were so angry that they threw me round the kitchen, my father grabbing one arm as my mother let go of the other. I bounced off the units. I was bruised all over. She was particularly good at being furious, slamming the prongs of her fork into a piece of potato at the dinner table, warningly looking away from me and saying nothing, and because the saying nothing was so much worse than the saying something I remember her saying:

I swear Iona, in a minute it'll be the back of my hand.

You'll be the death of me, girl.

You'll be sorry when I'm gone.

Then I remember something I haven't thought about for years. She was standing at the table flicking through a magazine and she held the magazine up and looked at me across the room. It was summer. I was sitting on the couch watching anything on TV. I was seventeen and sullen. She flapped the magazine in the air.

I think we should join this, she said.

It would be something about sewing or Catholicism or being more like a girl was supposed to be. I watched the TV as if something very important was on.

For only a penny each, she said, if you send to these people, you can get four books. A penny each. There are all these books you can choose from on this page. All you have to do is buy their Book of the Month. And then what they do, after that, they send you their Book of the Month every month for a year and you don't have to buy it if you don't want it. They have all these things you can choose from for a penny. The Collected Works of William Shakespeare. That would be a useful book for you to have.

What? I said, because I had been fighting for nearly a year to be allowed to do English at university, not Law or Languages but something that meant I would never have a proper job. I can see myself now coming across the room, my eyes wide, my face like a child's, or like someone whose hopelessly foreign language has suddenly been understood, and my mother pleased with herself, holding out the open page to me.

We ordered the Shakespeare collection and a dictionary and a thesaurus and a book of quotations.

Four weeks later they came all together in a box through the post and with them was the hardback Book Club Book of the Month which was called Princess Anne and her Horses and was full of colour photographs of Princess Anne and horses. My mother laughed and laughed. Then she saw the price of the book.

The following month the Book of the Month was a book about royal palaces. The month after that it was about the life of an English Edwardian lady. The month after that it was about the history of fox-hunting. They came every month, about gardens and the stately homes of members of royalty, always glossy with colour plates, expensive unwieldy hard-backs and my mother, who kept forgetting to send them back before the crucial eight days' return time, kept having to pay for them. They were stacked in the back room on the floor under the coffee table and there were more each time I came home at the end of a term.

I am wondering where all those useless books ended up, where they are now, whether they are still piled up unread somewhere in my father's house, when I hear the taxi driver speak. I open my eyes. The red light above his head is lit.

See how close we are, he says.

At the back of his voice the middle-class lady's voice is telling him to turn left in twenty yards.

Nearly home, he says.

Nearly home, I say.

He edges his cab between the cars parked on either side of the narrow roads before my own narrow road. He drives well.

You laughed in your sleep, he says. It must have been a good sleep.

He pulls up outside my house. It isn't as much on the meter as I thought it'd be. It is exactly the amount he told me it would be. I get the money out and count it and try to scrape together a good enough tip and I want to ask him, who called you Wasim? was it your mother or your father? is it after someone? does it mean something? what does it mean? I want to say, are you married? have you any children? are your parents still living? are they old enough to be supposed to be taking medication for anything and are they refusing to? did you grow up in Luton? what was it like to? what's it like there since Vauxhall closed and so many people lost their jobs? can we not just drive somewhere else, choose a place at random? could we go somewhere and not know where we're going till we got there? could we leave the navigation system off and just see where we ended up?

I get out of the cab and give him the money.

Thank you, I say.

Your book, he says. Don't forget.

I reach back in and pick it up off the seat.

He is looking at his watch now. Look, he says. We made good time. We took good roads. We were lucky.

He writes his number on the back of a receipt and I tell him I'll call him next time I need to come home. He drives up to the end of the road and round the corner, out of sight. I find my keys, unlock my front door, go in and close it behind me.

believe me

I'm having an affair, I said.

No you're not, you said.

It was Sunday morning. Outside was the sound of church bells and someone mowing a lawn; it was September; there wouldn't be many more lawnmowing days this year. I had made you coffee and you had gone out and brought home the croissants and then taken your clothes back off and left them on the floor and got back into bed beside me, as usual. You put your arms around my middle and rested your head against my back.

I am, I said. Don't you believe me?

You're not having an affair, you said behind me.

Actually, no, you're right, I said. I'm not having an affair. It's not an affair, it's much more than an affair. Actually I'm married to a man you've never met with whom I have three children you don't know about.

Ah, you said.

And every day when I leave the house and you think I'm going to work, actually I go to see my family.

You go to someone else's house –, you said.

Well, it's my house too –, I said.

And you stay there all day? you said. From half-past eight till six?

There's a lot to do there, I said. There's the clearing up after breakfast and the washing and the ironing and the making the beds and the cleaning the house –

Don't you have a home help? you said.

– and the getting lunch ready for them all coming back from school, now that the schools are back in, and making sure they leave the house on time and then clearing up after lunch and picking them up from school at 3.30 and seeing that they do their homework properly, and that's on the days when I don't do any shopping or have to look after Eric's mother, I said.

Who's Eric? you said.

Luckily I can do a lot of the food shopping online now, I said. That saves me an incredible amount of time, you wouldn't believe how much time. Occasionally I even have the chance to sit down by myself at the dining-room table in my other house and read a magazine or a bit of a book.

I can't believe you've got a dining-room table I don't know about, you said. I can't believe you haven't introduced me to your children. I would love to know your children. What are their names?

Ben is twelve, he's really good at skiing, I said. He won the school prize last year on their dry ski slope.

We were very proud of him when he got the certificate and the book at the prize-giving in June. We clapped like anything. We had real trouble finding a school that would understand him but Parkside seems to suit him. Academically he's a bit, well, recalcitrant, but they think he'll pick up, and we're getting him extra tuition, and he does love maths, like his father.

His father loves maths? you said.

Well, he did when he was at school apparently, I said.

But you hated maths, you said.

Opposites attract, I said, and then there's Amanda, Amanda is ten, she's a real, you know, bossy-boots, always telling the boys off, and she likes to perform, sing and dance, she's really very good, she's been taking tap lessons, her teacher says she's quite rhythmically advanced and I know she'll be running the school newspaper single-handedly soon, I'm sure she's going to end up being an important journalist one day, she's really very good with words.

That's only two, you said. There's another one.

The third's my baby, I said. Jonathan. He's seven.

He's your favourite, you said. I can tell by the way you talk about him.

Well, he's my baby, I said.

But how did you manage to keep them a secret from me for so long? you said.

I'm very discreet, I said.

You can't be discreet with pregnancy, you said. How did you keep three pregnancies hidden?

I ate very little, I said. I was very careful. I actually

lost weight when I was pregnant. And, well, you know the conferences I sometimes have to go away on for work?

What, when you go away for long weekends? you said.

Remember the one that was in Hawaii ten years ago –, I said.

The one that lasted a fortnight and you came back with jetlag? you said.

Difficult pregnancy, I said. Amanda. She was the wrong way up. They wanted to give me a Caesarean but I refused.

You didn't want a scar on your lovely abdomen, you said.

That's right, I said. How would I have explained a scar to you?

But what about that T-shirt you brought me back that says 'I love Honolulu'? you said.

It took a bit of organizing, but organizationally I'm very good, I said.

And how long have you been living this double life? you said.

Oh, just since the day you and I met, I said.

What, the whole time? you said. All those years?

I met my husband Eric the exact same day I met you, I said.

He's called Eric? you said.

Yes, his name's Eric, I said. What's wrong with that? Why are you laughing? I hope you're not laughing at the name Eric.

Eric's a really stupid name, you said, even for a fantasy character.

Eric isn't a fantasy character, I said. He's my husband. And if you knew Eric personally, like I do, you wouldn't think it was a stupid name.

And is Eric as good at this as I am? you said from under the covers as you kissed down across my stomach and slipped your arms under then over my thighs to hold me down.

I couldn't possibly compare you, I said after we'd surfaced, breathing evenly again, from you making love to me. I mean, how could I? Eric is my husband. You're my lover. You both fulfil different needs and roles.

I'm disappointed in you, you said sitting up. You're so unradical.

Unradical's not a word, I said.

I mean, listen, you said. You get the chance to invent another life for yourself and what do you do?

What do you mean, invent? I said. I'm not inventing anything.

You could have been anyone, you said, anyone in the world. You could have been a, a superheroine. You could have worked for MI5, or the government.

What? Me, tell lies? I said.

You could have been a cat burglar, or someone who ran away and joined a circus and trained elephants to put their feet on beach balls, or, I don't know, a friend and confidante of the rich and famous who helped Kim Basinger out with her problems and got that man who's on television out of jail and into drug rehabilitation –

What man? I said.

I don't know his name, you said, he went to jail, he's on that programme with the thin woman.

What thin woman? I said.

That TV programme I hate, you said. Never mind him. My point is: you could have been an important peacekeeping force at the UN. You could have been the doctor who is working to discover the cure for BSE in humans before it gets us all. But no. A husband. Three children. A mother-in-law, for God's sake.

I'm telling you, I said. Elaine is a real pain in the neck.

Who's Elaine? you said.

My mother-in-law, I said, and you'll never believe the lies she tells Er about me.

Tells who? you said.

Er, I said. Short for Eric.

You swore and slapped the bedclothes with both your hands. Much more of this and I'm going to go mad, you said.

I am too if she tells him that lie any more about me being a secret alcoholic drinking by myself all day in the house, I said, I'm sure she phones him at night when I'm not there and winds him up. I'm sure she's told him I'm having an affair. I'm sure she's on at him to take the children and leave me. Not that Er would believe her, though.

No, you said, because he trusts you, doesn't he?

Well, I don't mean to boast but we do know each other very well, I said. But the last time I looked at the whisky decanter, I swear it wasn't just dust, I swear there was a thin chalkline round the outside, you know, marking the level. And you know when you pick up the phone and you can hear a little click –

That little click that means that someone else might be listening to what you're saying? you said. Is that the little click you mean?

That's it, I said. So you can see the kind of woman she is. She never liked me. Not since the day I married him.

I can't believe I'm even in bed with you, you said. You are such a cliché it's not true.

It is true, I said. All of it. You know I never lie.

And where do Eric and Ben and Amanda and Jonathan and Elaine think you are now? you said. Where do they think you are every night, and every weekend, and on Christmases and Easters and bank holidays?

I'm a busy woman, I said. I'm a modern girl. They know I've got a life to lead.

I was just wondering, you said.

What? I said.

Your Eric, you said. What does he look like?

Why? I said.

Don't be so suspicious, you said. For instance, has he got a little moustache?

Oh no, I said, not my Er.

Yes, that's right, you said. Neither has my one. Is he balding and a little overweight?

Absolutely not, I said. My Er is in the prime of his life.

I thought so, you said.

What do you mean? I said. And what do you mean, neither has *your one* got a moustache?

I've got something to tell you, you said.

What? I said.

I'm having an affair, you said.

No, you're not, I said.

With a man called Eric, you said. I'm pretty sure from your description that it's the same Eric.

My Eric? I said.

Well, he's my Eric too, you said.

No way, I said.

I've known Ric since we were kids, you said. We were at school together. I remember how he loved maths. We grew up together, then our lives took different paths. He's a family man now.

There is no way you're taking over my other life, I said.

We meet during the day when his wife thinks he's at work, you said. His mother, Elaine, she'll be elderly now; she was a friend of my mother's, you know, they used to smoke cigarettes and stand and laugh with each other at the back doors of the houses on the council estate we lived on –

Ah. Now. My Er didn't grow up on a council estate –, I said.

Ric always lies about it, he was so ashamed of our upbringing, you said. Everything is very fragile with him, he lives a lie.

What do you mean? I said.

144

Well, his wife for instance, you said.

What about her? I said.

Well, I worry for her, you said. Her husband having an affair. Alone in the house all day drinking by herself, or stuck with those horrible children. The eldest boy's practically a juvenile delinquent –

He's what? I said.

All that business with the police and the correction home, you said, and his sister's no better, she's only ten and she was caught shoplifting vodka from Oddbins and when the police brought her home they said they'd never met such a foulmouthed child, she got out of the car in her ballet tutu and she was swearing swears at them, I swear I've never heard before some of the swears she used, they were so obscene. And that little one. The 'baby', they call him.

What about him? I said.

Well, he's the baby, you said. He's the mother's favourite, you know. He's her image. He's nothing like his father. Because, to tell you the truth, the thing about my relationship with Ric.

Is? I said.

Well, I think if I were to admit the truth, you said.

Uh huh? I said.

I'd have to say, you said, that the only reason I still have anything to do with him is his wife.

His wife? I said.

She's so beautiful, you said. She's so lovely. To be honest, I'm hopelessly in love with his wife. I only stay close to Ric so I can stay close to her. She's a woman full of potential. I'm sure she's a person capable of so many other things.

Given the chance, I said.

Exactly, you said.

We made love. We spent the rest of the morning making it, then some of the afternoon. We began when you pressed my thighs apart with a pressure so subtle and so sure that it caught me by surprise and stopped me in mid-sentence, I breathed in, and you slid between them and traced with your tongue the thin line of hairs on my stomach leading down to my groin, then shifted up and fully on to me and kissed me openly, with skill, because you know me so well, and then me on you because I can read you like a book and because the thing about a beloved book, if it's a good one, is that it shifts like music; you think you know it, you've read it so many times, of course you know it, of course the pleasure of it is in how well you know it, but then you hear, in the background, the thing you never heard in it before, and with the turn of a page you see a combination of words you know you've never seen before, you thought you knew this book but it dazzles you with the different book it is, yet again, and not just that but the different person you have become, the different person you are now, reading it again, and you, my love, are an excellent book for me, and then us both together, which takes some talent with rhythm, but luckily we are quite talented at reading each other.

We made love all morning and some of the

afternoon. The hours passed. Outside the leaves on the trees constricted slightly; they were the deep done green of the beginning of the autumn. It was a Sunday in September. There would only be four. The clouds were high and the swallows would be here for another month or so before they left for the south before they returned again next summer.

scottish love songs

Violet was being haunted by a pipe band in full regalia. There had never been so many burly men about the house and not one of them needing feeding. They swished their kilts through the front room, scraped the tall stems of their bagpipes against the ceiling and knocked their bearskins squint on the doorframes and the pelmets. They sent ornaments flying. They made the decanter and glasses shiver in the cabinet. They paraded up and down the stairs and rumpled the rug on the landing. They disturbed the bedroom curtains and left the pictures hanging askew.

They came at all hours of the day and night and they always played the same tune. The whole house shook with it. It shook even after they'd left. Violet's hand shook as she bent down, slow because it was sore to bend down, and picked up the robin again, the chaffinches on their branch, the young courting couple one on either side of the stile. She put them back in their places. She went up the stairs, she felt the creak beneath her feet but she couldn't hear the creak. She straightened the pictures. She saw her reflection in the glass of the picture of the birds on the water. She was looking ten years younger. Well well well, she said out loud to herself. But it was like speaking out loud next to a waterfall; she couldn't hear anything beyond the tune going round and round in her head. It was sad. It was good. It was what you'd call rousing. On the landing she bent down and straightened the rug. Then she straightened herself up again and went back down the stairs.

A girl who Violet didn't know had also taken to visiting her. She came in a bus all the way out to Dalston. She was young and not married yet and so had nothing better to do. She always brought Violet a cake or a packet of biscuits from the expensive shops where she lived. She was clearly a girl who had never known hunger. Here she was at the door again.

What do you want now? Violet said.

The girl was a pest. She was a free service for elderly people. She had the good clear way the skin is and the prettiness of the well-off. Anyway Violet couldn't hear a thing she said.

They sat round the fire in the front room.

You'll not get the good of that, wearing it inside, Violet shouted.

The girl took her jacket off.

You'll be cold, Violet shouted, switching on another bar.

The girl took her jumper off too. She was young and

warmed up easily. She went and made a pot of tea in Violet's kitchen and brought it through on the tray with cups and the things from the expensive shops out on plates.

The girl and the pipe band were not Violet's only visitors. She could get the doctor to visit if she needed to by shouting down the phone. Her daughter came round several times a month, sometimes with her husband and sometimes without. When she came alone she read the property section of the local paper or went round the house lifting things up and looking at them and putting them back down. Violet watched her sitting there across the room counting the number of glasses in the cabinet. You can tell it's crystal when you ping it with your finger, Violet had taught her when she was a little girl. After Violet married the house was always full of glass. The sixties and the seventies were a real time of coloured glass. I wish she would get up and open the cabinet and ping the crystal with her finger now, Violet thought; she closed her eyes in the wake of the endless tune and imagined her daughter rising out of the chair, sliding the glass door back in its groove, choosing one wineglass, removing it without nudging any of the others, holding it up by the stem near her ear like the forks they used to tune pianos, getting her finger ready to give it the hint of a flick, just, to test if it was true. But when she opened her eyes her daughter hadn't moved an inch. Now she was eyeing the hostess trolley next to the cabinet. She pointed at it. Her mouth moved. She was saying something.

Have it, Violet said, waving her away like waving away a fly. Take it, it's yours.

Her daughter's husband these days was a man whose job was making things in his garage. Every time Violet had to go and visit them he was in the garage making things. Whenever he came to Violet's house he stood by the door or leaned on the back of the chair being patient while she spoke to Violet more than she did when she came alone. Not that Violet could hear anyway, nothing in her ears now but the pipes, fainter if the band wasn't still in the house, loud if it was, and not that her daughter or the husband even noticed it at all; they were deaf and blind to it and last Wednesday the pipers, who though they were a smartly sporranned and gartered lot still looked like they'd been through a war or two, had figure-of-eighted under both their noses in the kitchenette providing a gallant accompaniment to them standing over the table reading the life insurance leaflet that someone had put through the doors of the road that Violet lived in. Violet had laughed, clapping her hands out in front of her. The daughter and her husband had exchanged glances. They thought she was old and mad. Violet pointed at the chipped ornaments on the sideboard. Look, she shouted. They went back to reading the leaflet. You could get £80,000, if you died.

Violet blinked awake. It wasn't her daughter here in the chair today, it was that girl. She had been here all afternoon. She was young enough to curl her legs right under her in the chair, like a cat that lived here. Violet

had no idea why she was here. She had been to visit
many times but Violet didn't even know her name.

The girl saw Violet watching her. She uncurled her
legs. She sat up.

You ever been there? Violet said.

The girl didn't understand.

I said Canada, Violet said louder. You ever been to
Canada?

The girl shook her head.

Not been to the place with the falls? Violet said. A
rich girl like you that could go anywhere she wanted in
the world?

The girl smiled.

Oh I'm telling you. The noise off those falls is louder
than anything. You can hear them from miles away.
Miles away we were and we heard them. When we
were stood right on the edge I couldn't hear a thing. So
I can say I saw a wonder of the world. And I can also
say I heard a wonder of the world. How many people
are there can say that then? Out of all the millions of
people there are in the world. Nineteen fifty-three.
They had a place for the dancing. You know?

The girl nodded.

I could have been a different person, Violet said. The
other side of the world.

The girl's mouth opened and made the shape of a
yes.

You should go, Violet said.

The girl nodded and piled the plates and cups
together on the tray.

No, I don't mean go now, I mean go there, go to
Canada, that place, what's it called? Violet said.

The girl smiled and looked at her watch. She lifted
the tray and all the things slid together to one side. She
was no good at knowing what to do with a tray. Violet
watched the things silently clatter as they hit into one
another but all there was was the noise they were
making upstairs, the noise air could make coming out
of an old leather lung, noise in the shape of a tune that
shook the heart. Was it leather the bag was made of on
bagpipes? She didn't know. It was tough, anyway. It
could take a lot. They were playing somewhere close,
overhead, directly above in the bedroom maybe or
maybe up in the loft with all the photographs in the
boxes and the piled-up stuff Violet wouldn't ever see
again. They could kick it back to make room for
themselves if they liked. They could make any mess
they wanted. Violet didn't mind.

That girl had come back into the living room again.
She was pulling on her jumper. Her time at Violet's
house was up.

My daughter's name is Jean, Violet said. I named her
after Jean Simmons. You won't have heard of Jean
Simmons.

The girl's ponytail reappeared out of the top of her
jumper.

She was an actress, Jean Simmons, Violet said.

The girl said something. She rummaged about in the
pocket of her jacket and brought out something. It was
a little book. It was the size of her hand. She flipped it

open in the middle. Its pages were blank. She fished about in her other pocket for a pen and wrote something down and showed it to Violet. Violet took the book and held it up close to her eyes. The girl had written the place she was from. Violet had known the insides of a lot of the houses there. She had cleaned for people who had money. They would all be different people in them now.

The place I just told you about, Violet said. I can't remember the name.

The girl took the book back and wrote something down again. Violet squinted at it; under the word Chelsea it said: Canada. Violet pushed the book away in the girl's hand.

No, she said. The place, the town where the water is. I can't remember the name.

The girl wrote something else. She showed Violet the page, two more words with a question mark after them. Niagara   Falls   ?

That's it, Violet said. That's it. Niagara. Right on the edge and all that water. Smooth on the top like simmering and then it all falls away. It'll be the same to this day. When you see it you can't believe it, that people went over that edge in a barrel and survived, or fell in and were still living when they reached the bottom, but they did and they were, some of them. Not all of them. Now, she said. Listen. She took hold of the girl by the arm because the girl had looked at her watch again.

What, the girl's mouth said, or who, or wait.

Violet sat herself up as straight as she could. She

coughed. She swallowed. She cleared her throat. She waited for where her boys up above would get back to the start of their nimble lament again. She tapped her foot to count herself in and she sang the song to the rich girl.

Chelsea's friend Amanda had appeared to Chelsea in a dream in the middle of the night, wearing no clothes. It was not the only dream Chelsea had had like this. She walked along the leafy white-housed roads (Chelsea lived in Chelsea) and thought hard of other things. She thought about aerodynamics. She thought about the contents of nitrogen and oxygen in air. She thought about how Mrs Waterman shouted all the time, like she was shouting across a ravine. She thought how it was spring on the other side of the world, winter was finished over there and just about to start here in this unnatural warm. It was far too warm for this time of year. She thought about what would happen if global warming continued destabilizing the climate. She thought about the pond in the middle of Hyde Park. She thought about how microbes breathe in water. She thought about how Amanda was a microbiologist. Once she had sent Chelsea a text message from the middle of a river saying AM STNDN IN MDDLE OF TAY WEARING FULL BIOHZARD SUIT FRM HD TO TOE!! LV TO Y FRM ME + MANY LIFEFORMS. That was last year, when Amanda was still here. With no clothes on Amanda was sitting crosslegged on her futon and looking straight at

Chelsea. Chelsea had woken up in the middle of the night wet, saying the word no. Troposphere tropopause ozone layer stratosphere, she thought as she pushed the door of the deli open. The deli was a very good one. It had an excellent reputation. Stratopause mesosphere mesopause thermospere aurora. The atmosphere had a structure. Chelsea knew the correct names for its levels.

A lot of men in kilts were in the deli queueing behind Chelsea. When she left the deli, they left too. They were right behind her. She stopped in the middle of the pavement and turned round. They brayed their noise right at her. She laughed politely. They looked mud-spattered, they were grandly dressed, yet they looked as though they'd been sleeping rough.

She checked her purse for change. She put a couple of pounds down on the pavement by the big-buckled shoe of one of the men and signalled thank you. He ignored it. He more than ignored it; he turned his beard up at it. He was offended. Maybe they were more official than they seemed. Possibly they were something to do with the V&A.

But they marched squealing and wailing straight past the doors of the museum and they followed her all along the Brompton Road. She began to jog a little. She started to run. She dodged tourists and she crossed the road dodging the fast-coming cars. She ducked into Harrods. The doorman held the door open. They wouldn't be allowed. But in they came, still following her, still making the awful noise. No security person did anything to help. They followed her through the Food Halls. They followed her through Jewellery. She doubled back and so did they; they crowded up the escalator behind her. She faced forward, innocent, staring straight ahead with one hand on the moving handbelt. But they were there squeeing and squawing and baying and bawing and heeing and hawing through Books then Toys then Leather Goods. They were following her down the stairs and out of the shop as if she were their bandmaster. They strutted behind her into Knightsbridge tube station where she lost them by ducking through the luggage gate.

It was the airport train. She sat in the first seat she came to. She held her breath. They would still be fumbling about at the top for change for the ticket machines, trying to squeeze themselves and their uniforms and instruments through the automatic ticket barriers. The train left. A man opposite was reading his newspaper. A woman next to him stared unfocussed at nothing. Chelsea opened the box to check the sushi was still all right. She shut the box and she shut her eyes. The train ran on to the next stop and the doors opened and she heard the brazen yelp of them coming from the carriage behind or ahead of her, and the doors closed. The man read his paper as if nothing was happening. The woman stared ahead at nothing. Another woman stared ahead at nothing. A woman along the carriage read a paper. Another read a book. A couple of people stood swaying with the train by the door. Two tourists in shorts leaned on a rucksack. Chelsea looked at the filthy floor. It had grey-white specks in its linoleum, like a fake starry sky beneath her feet. At every stop the doors opened, people got off and other people got on and the noise of them behind or ahead of her echoed beyond the train out into the network of tunnels.

They played the same tune over and over out to Heathrow then back and after that they followed Chelsea off the tube and up the road still playing it.

Would any of you like a cup of coffee or tea yet? Chelsea said again some hours later.

The pipers were standing playing in a circle round the coffee table in the lounge. This was where they'd been standing since they'd battered their way through the front door. The door was still flung open. Their chests rose and fell as they took in breath and expended it. They breathed their different rhythms, all playing the same tune. The tartan-webbed bits of the pipes, resting against their shoulders, stuck out like branches. It was as if a copse of lopsided breathing trees had grown from nowhere out of the floor of her mother's flat. Talking to them was as pointless as talking to trees. Can I get you anything? Chelsea had asked. Are you planning on staying long? Where else have you played? Have any of you been travelling? Have any of you been to Australia? I was there recently, I spent some time in Melbourne, do any of you know Melbourne?

The men had ignored her like they were ignoring her now. Oh for fuck sake, Chelsea thought. She was mildly fearful that they might all do something unpleasant that would foul the carpet and the walls and she'd have to clean up after them. But she was a polite person so what she said out loud was: I also have several kinds of herbal tea. Or I could open a bottle of wine. Can I get anyone anything to eat?

They looked anywhere but at her. They looked, if anything, contemptuous. Their cheeks filled with air and gradually emptied and filled again. Every breath went into the pipes which more and more resembled something alive, long-snouted and implacable with three legs in the air as if in a butcher's shed strung up for slaughter; if left to sit by themselves on the floor, she knew, they would scuttle about blind and panicking, horrifyingly uneven, asphyxiating like sea creatures in the wrong element.

She pushed the front door shut; its hinges were warped from the forced entry. She went to the kitchen and made herself a cup of tea. She poked at the sushi, still in its box. She had no appetite. Outside it was raining and the dark came early. She stood in the kitchen, leaned on the breakfast bar and tried to read a book. But she couldn't concentrate; the noise they were making was monstrous. She switched the radio on but the noise was too loud for it. She switched it off again. She switched the television on and used text to get subtitles, but subtitles were only available on channels she didn't want to watch. She switched it off again.

She went through to the lounge.

Please stop, she said.

The pipers carried on breathing hard.

You bastards, she said. Get out of my mother's house.

They puffed. They blew. They avoided her eye. Their avoidance of it was scornful.

She thought about phoning social services and asking them what to do when a lot of poor-looking people from another country took up residence in your property. She didn't know which department to ask for. Instead she phoned her mother who was staying in a hotel in Helsinki.

? her mother said.

I can hardly hear you, Chelsea said.

You woke me, her mother said. Time, for God's sake. What do you want?

What? Chelsea said.

What? her mother said. Poor connection. I can hardly hear you.

You'll have to speak up, Chelsea said.

Was there anything? her mother said.

Chelsea held the phone away from her in the air, angled towards the lounge where the noise was. She held it there for ten seconds then she put the phone to her ear again.

Hello? her mother said. Hello hello hello hello?

Hello? Chelsea said into the receiver.

I said, was there anything you actually wanted? her mother said.

Never mind, Chelsea said.

What? her mother said.

It's okay, Chelsea said.

Things are fine here, her mother said. I'll let you know if I need anything. Make sure you pay the floor-polisher bill, it's £163, take it out of the cash. And your father's suits need to be picked up from Arcadia and so do my things, there are seven different things altogether of mine there and could you check with him how many of his suits? And could you ask Maria to clear out the guttering?

Okay, Chelsea said. She had no real idea what her mother was saying. It was probably about the dry cleaning, which she had already collected. Lots of love, her mother said inaudibly from her hotel in Finland. Bye, Chelsea said from the flat in London. She hung up. She lifted the receiver and dialled and pushed the phone as close to her ear as she could and put her finger hard into the hole of her other ear and she could hear that thousands of miles away the phone was ringing then the voice was on the answerphone, no distance away. The message was merry. It made Chelsea feel worse. She listened to it all the way to its end, listened to the nothing she was leaving in the space allotted for her own message and then hung up the phone again.

She went through and sat on the couch. The tune they were playing grew on you. It was angry but it was loving. It was boisterous and gentle. It was full of loss and hope.

Chelsea noticed that their naked knees beneath their kilts were massive. Their hands were red-raw from playing. The one nearest her had perspiration running down his face. They all did. It must be hard work, putting every breath into playing those things and playing them endlessly, wearing those great fur hats and heavy-looking jackets in a centrally-heated room.

When the pipers reached the end again, Chelsea gave in. She applauded.

Bravo, she said.

The man nearest Chelsea almost smiled. The pipers signalled to each other over her head with nods and winks. They began the noise again at the beginning.

In the middle of the night they were sitting all round her on the couch, on the arms of the couch, on the coffee table, on the chairs, on the floor. The working day was over. One of them was singing. Though it was harder to tell now that they had their bearskin hats off, she thought he might be the one who had seemed most disdainful earlier. If my true love she'll not come, he sang. Then I'll surely find another.

It was a sad song about a wild time on a mountain. They all joined in at the chorus. At the end they cheered and clapped and clinked their glasses. The man with the beard, sitting next to Chelsea, started to sing. His face was deep red from working and drinking. He sang about how his sweetheart had promised him true, how he would lie down and die for her, so pretty she was, with her dark blue eyes and her face the fairest the sun had ever shone on.

The small dark wounded-looking one sang about a man meeting a girl by chance on a road. She asks him how far to the city it is and which road to take and out of courtesy, and because the girl is so lovely, he goes out of his way and accompanies her. When they can see the spires of the city in the distance she thanks him. He gives her a gold pin from his coat and kisses her, and she's gone. She appeared like an angel in feature and form as she walked by my side, he sang.

Chelsea was broken by the song. At last she wept. At last the men looked pleased. They looked grave. They looked loyal. The one with the beard put his arm round Chelsea and gave her a wet kiss on the mouth. He smelt and tasted of whisky, or blood.

Later, near dawn, she walked out to the park to get some air. The pipers followed her, two by two. She sat on a bench by the deserted autumn water and watched the birds rising and landing. The pipe band stood a little way off and played ceremoniously, one last time, as the morning came up round London.

He was a Scottish boy and was working on a farm in Ontario. He'd signed up for the army underage at the end of the war and ended up in Canada after it and just stayed. I was nineteen. It was the land of opportunity and my mother, she saved the fare for me, she was half-Scottish herself, she had family out in Banff, her little sister, it was supposed to be a better life. But the whole time I was there I wanted my home. I was on my way home when I met him. He was sat across from me on the bus to the east, I liked the look of him, we got talking. When we got to the city we went to a picture, it was Affair With A Stranger, then he said he'd take me the next day to see a wonder of the world. We got there and you couldn't hear a thing! The water of it was that loud. The spray was in the air, we were covered in it from just standing there, it was all in my hair. He wanted me to stay and we would have our own farm, the farms were huge over there, much bigger than here. But I was on my way home, I had my ticket and I didn't know anything about farms, I had grown up in the city and anyway I wasn't for marrying yet. The year after I got back home my mother died and the year after that I married a man I met at a Railways dance, he was a salesman, he sold glass.

the shortlist season

It was the turn of the century, and the turn of the season again. I had been to the bank and now I was at a loss, so I crossed the park to get to the contemporary art gallery where an exhibition which had been written up in all the papers as culturally important was still showing.

The city was blowing about that day in the dregs of a storm which was happening (or had maybe already happened) thousands of miles away across the Atlantic; in the far distance over the park a tractor was spreading fertilizer on its lawns against the damage that winter would do. I walked under the trees. Leaves, fast and hardened, scuffed against my head and grazed my face. In front of me on the path a man was collecting fallen leaves; he looked ridiculous, large for the machine he sat on which was whirring at the too-high pitch of a full domestic vacuum cleaner as he sucked leaves up through its nozzle, and more were falling behind him, in front of me, on the paths he'd already cleared. Leaves blew round us like birds, or painted snow. When I reached the gallery I had to brush smaller leaves off my shoulders.

Outside the front door a man was talking to some younger men. The wind blew his hair the wrong way and he held it in place with one hand, waving his other hand about. The younger men's deference to him and the angle of his back, the bend of his head on his neck, all meant the man was an authority on something. *Of course, it has its own inherent narrative*, he was saying, *but its narrative is*.

Its narrative is. But I don't know what. I couldn't make out the rest, and if I'd walked any more slowly or turned to stand and listen then the three men would have sensed me and I would have made them uneasy. Someone, a mad person maybe, or at least a slightly dangerously incalculable person (the city being full of them) would have been listening in to their private conversation in an uncalled-for way. Wind-charred now in the warm gallery foyer I pulled my sweater over my head, and it was a little irritating to me, the fact that I could so easily have seemed mad or like one of those incalculable people to them. Mostly though, I thought with my mouth full of wool, I was irritated because I wouldn't, because I won't – ever – know what came after that man's *is*, or what exactly it was he was talking about, what he meant by saying the words he did, what he knew the inside story to be.

There were leaves caught in the hood of my sweater.

Something fell out. When it hit the floor it bounced
quite high and made a surprisingly sharp noise for such
a small thing, and I picked it up. It was a sycamore
seed, its single propeller was veined like a kind of skin
and made the seed surreal: a small flying hazelnut, a
wing with a shrunken head attached, a fish almost all
fin. But the gallery assistant behind the postcard
counter was watching me with a kind of interest so I
put the seed back inside my sweater with the leaves,
folded it over my arm and listened politely as he told
me that entry was free, handouts about the exhibition
were also free and illustrated catalogues were £16.50.

Usually the people who work behind the counters of
galleries like this one are supercilious about the people
who come to see the art, but this assistant was new,
still unjaded, keen. I let him tell me all of it, the price of
the smaller postcards, the price of the larger ones and
the ones with three-dimensional effects, and the fact
that the posters were sold out but the reorder would be
in any day. I opened a display catalogue at a photograph of two cups of coffee on a coffee table; I flicked
through it, closed it and put it back on the pile of other
catalogues sealed inside cellophane. The assistant was
holding out a piece of paper. It was a competition
leaflet with a picture of a car on it, organized, it said, in
tandem with the exhibition. If I filled in my name and
address, allowed a car company to put my name on a
mailing list for junk mail and could say in no more
than ten words why I thought modern art mattered, I
might win a car. You can fill it in later, the assistant

told me, and leave it here on your way out. Or you could fill it in now if you like. You could borrow my pen.

He was beginning to annoy me. He was smiling a great deal. He was acting as if he knew me. I put the leaflet in my pocket, thanked him and took a handout.

Or maybe if I *had* stopped to listen to those three men talking outside, I was thinking as I pushed through the swing doors to the exhibition, maybe they wouldn't have been uneasy at all, maybe they'd have been secretly pleased, because it is always nice, one way or another, to think that someone somewhere is listening. Maybe they'd have smirked self-consciously and nodded to me to join their group, made space for me. The man holding forth might even have conceded to explain. *What I'm talking about is*. Or: *I'm referring to the manner in which the*. Who knew? I went round the gallery and looked at the pictures, the sculptures and the installations.

They had been created by male twins now in their forties, who'd been born siamese but separated soon after birth. The twins and their art were very fashionable; this exhibition, it announced on a board on the wall, had placed them on the prestigious shortlist of a current art award. Broadsheet newspapers were full of authoritative lists and shortlists just now; the best films and pop songs and historical moments of the century, the best music of the year, best novel, best poetry collection, best art. Papers had been running pictures of these twins taken just after they'd been separated and of them as they were now, beside pictures of their sculptures or paintings and stills from their videos. The odds on them winning the art award were short, something like 3/1. I walked around the rooms in the too-hot gallery; though there were several people walking and stopping like me we were all respectful, subdued, like people generally are at a gallery, as if in a church or a bookshop. But I was sweating. Sweat was running down my back; I could feel it the length of my spine. I put my hand behind my neck just under my hairline and it came away wet. I stood in the middle of the gallery and looked at the sweat on my fingers.

It was because of the change in temperature between outside and in, or the larger temperature changes that happen in the change of a season. Or maybe, I thought as I laughed at myself inside my head and wiped my hand on my shirt, the reason I was sweating was because I would never know how the man at the door had finished his sentence. I felt a little dizzy. I felt weak. I began to wonder whether I'd caught some horrible flu virus, or something worse, something with no name which was right now multiplying itself through the inside of me. I glanced at a man who was going past me looking at the art in the wrong direction, the other way round from the way suggested by the arrows stencilled at the front door. For instance, he looked fine. He didn't seem to be sweating. He didn't even look hot. Nobody else in the room looked hot.

I stopped beside a sculpture of a coffee table with

cups on it which were half-full of something rust-coloured, a folded newspaper placed next to them. The cups had what looked like perspex fixed over their tops and the newspaper's pages were stapled together with thin metal staples all the way round it. I walked on. I could feel my legs beneath me. I kept walking at the right art gallery pace; I didn't want to seem unusual to anyone. The only sound in the rooms was occasional and came from the video installations; it was an inter-mittent grinding noise, like teeth in the mouth of a sleeping person recorded very close-up, or something industrial. The video screens took up three walls of a darkened room; I watched for a while but couldn't tell what it was I was looking at. On all three walls there was something red and dark and its surface shifted, shone dully; perhaps it was the massive inside of a mouth, a tongue laid flat on a palate bone. Now I could feel my mouth, cavernous, and the way my jaw raised its bone up and became the bottom row of my teeth. I came out of the dark. I concentrated on the paintings instead.

They were uniformly huge and square, each reaching from the skirting board up to the edge of the ceiling and each pair filling a wall as if this gallery, designed at the turn of the last century, had been planned especially to fit these paintings. They were all in pairs. The first of the pairs was of something recognizable and domestic, say a teapot or a dog. The second was a near-empty canvas, cleanish, always smudged at the centre like the painter had touched it there by chance with a hand not clean enough. The images together would be titled: Teapot, 1 & 2 or: Dog, 1 & 2.

I got it. It didn't exactly take long to get. It was all about alienation and distance, wasn't it? I had only had to walk once round the gallery, which is pretty small, to get it, but I walked round a couple more times just to prove to myself that in this sweating state I could. After the third time I stopped and sat breathing on a stool in the corner, the kind that the art gallery attendants usually sit on.

The two paintings opposite me now were called Road, 1 & 2. The one on the left was of an empty tarmacked road leading into middle distance with plain grass verges on either side of it. The one on the right was another canvas left almost completely empty behind its glass, just the clay-coloured smudge at its centre resembling grime or a mistaken touch. On the front of the free handout it told me that the twins liked to *paint two identical works then slowly, painstakingly, to remove all paint from one of the paired canvases except for a scant trace at the centre of the gone image*, and as soon as I read this I remembered I'd already known that this was what the twins did, that I had read about this process in a Sunday newspaper or somewhere similar.

I felt shopsoiled, cheated on by my own memory. I sat back on the stool, leaned my weight into the wall behind me and closed my eyes. Then I remembered: the last time I had visited an art exhibition, several months back, I had also felt so unwell that I had had to sit down. It had been at a bigger, grander gallery in the middle of the city. At the very top of the building, up several flights of stairs and along a corridor lined in marble so glassy you could see yourself reflected from the feet up as you walked along it, there were three rooms filled with the small, relentless, brightly coloured pictures a painter had used to record the various stories of her life and her family's lives in Berlin in the thirties and forties before her death, inevitable, pregnant and statistical. That day, I recalled now, I had been able to look closely at only three of the hundreds of her paintings before feeling the floor under my feet start to shift and creak like the whole of the gallery beneath us – beneath all these people wandering round the rooms and listening to the story of the paintings on the hired gallery CD machines hung at their waists, the CDs whirring in small circles unimaginable to anyone when the pictures were painted – was a ship on a pitching ocean and us in its crow's-nest swaying and dipping.

I had rocked in one place on my heels and toes to keep myself upright, my face disinterested, until someone, a lady, pushed herself up off the padded seat in the middle of the floor, and her getting up made room for me. Then I had sat in the same room and counted the strips of wood in the floor, examining the varnished dust and stuff trapped in the spaces between them, the paintings still there, raucous colour hovering above my eye-line, until the bell for closing rang and a man in a uniform came round telling everybody to leave, and I could go.

Perhaps it was art that made me sweat. Perhaps sculptures and pictures were inherently bad for me. I suppressed a laugh. It was funny. Earlier that morning I had been to the bank which gave me my mortgage; for some reason the woman behind the counter there is always telling me stories of infirmities and deaths. She is always having inconclusive tests, usually for something frightening. Perhaps, I thought to myself, I could have tests for art intolerance, like patch tests. *We have the results*, the doctor would say. *You are sensitive to dust-mites, the hairs of cats and horses, shellfish, metals related to nickel, and several forms of cultural expression.* I would breathe a sigh of relief. I would discover, not too late, that my life could have been symptom-free and simple all along, a matter of deep, healthy, fluid-free breaths if only I'd known to not go near art. After that I would visit theatres and galleries and cinemas and bookshops drowsily, in the haze of antihistamines, my senses so blunt that I wouldn't care in the slightest what the inherent narrative was or might be.

I always seem to get that woman serving me at the bank. Canadian, dark and thin, she has frail unsunned skin; her face through the saliva-specked double-reinforced glass is always pale. That morning, before I had felt so suddenly at a loss and had decided to take the day off work and spend some time at the contemporary art gallery, she told me a sad story while she added up my cheques. A bank colleague, only thirty-three, in fact only thirty-three last week. Year and a half ago a lump in her arm size of a small satsuma. Size of a clementine. Operated on. Given the all-clear. Six weeks ago terrible headaches. Went back to hospital. Riddled all through. Died yesterday. Only thirty-three. Imagine. Divorced. Daughter aged four who had said to other bank colleague called Mary who was visiting, Mummy is in the hospital and might not be coming back.

I nodded from the other side, said things, signed the paying-in slip, put it in the hollow space banks have for passing things through. My heart had grown bulky inside me one more time; one more time I was resolving behind my sympathetic face to change my branch. The woman was pressing something up against the inside glass layer at me, a grainy photograph, faxed or photocopied, of some people smiling at a party or in a pub. That's the woman who died on the right, she was saying; did I recognize her? The faces were inky and shadowed and the picture bleeding to white in the several folds and creases in the copy; it had been through many hands. *So do something frivolous*, the woman had shouted after me through the glass as I left the bank. *Be sure and do something frivolous today*.

Something frivolous: I had gone to an art gallery. I was sweating. I was sitting on a stool in an art gallery with my eyes shut.

I opened them and I saw a small girl of perhaps three or four smiling at me. When I smiled back, she stopped smiling and hid round the back of the legs of her mother who was standing in the middle of the room

talking in a polite hush to another woman. The child
swung round her mother's legs, pinning them both with
her arms. She let go. She flung herself into the middle of
the floor. She jumped from square to square of stone.
She ignored *Road 2* and stood in front of *Road 1*.
Launching herself at the road as if she were about to
run down it, she hit the picture, flat, with the weight of
her whole body. The picture shuddered on the wall.
The child made an amazed noise. She stood back and
touched her nose.

Ow, she said.

Oh God, the mother said. Oh God, Sophie. Oh.

She turned to me. I'm so sorry, she said. I'm sorry.
She just. Sorry.

No, I said, I'm not the. I mean. I'm –.

I stood up. Now the mother was rubbing with a
tissue at the two clear prints her daughter's hands had
made on the glass. She was laughing, embarrassed,
swearing under her breath. Sophie, she said.

No, I said. Don't – Please don't touch the paintings.

Oh, the woman said. Right. I'm sorry.

She stepped back, stood holding the tissue in the air,
not knowing what to do. She put it in her bag. She
turned, pretty and flustered, and exchanged a glance
with her friend who was holding the child by the shoulders
and smiling, eyes lowered not to laugh, looking down
at the top of the child's head. The child was singing
something impenetrable, doing a dance again.

It's okay, I said. It's just that we can't, you know,
have anyone touching the paintings.

177

I'm really sorry, the woman said again. Come on, Sophie, we've to go now.

Both women made to gather the child into an anorak.

No, you can remain in the gallery, I said. It's fine. But just, well. Just don't let it happen again.

The woman relaxed. She was thanking me. But a real attendant was coming over, so I smiled what I imagined was a stern, official, goodbye kind of smile to the women, and turned to go. So that they wouldn't realize, I stopped the attendant as he passed and asked him quietly when the gallery closed. The women behind me with the child would think he was giving me orders about work, or perhaps that I was giving them to him.

The attendant looked at me with the eyes and the hauteur of someone who knows everything there is to know. But it was all right. He didn't know anything. The gallery closes at six tonight, he said.

Thanks, I said. And when does the exhibition finish?

This exhibition closes on the thirtieth, he said.

I strolled through the room whose walls could have been the insides of someone's mouth, and out the other side. I pulled my sweater on over my head. I didn't care. I was feeling better. I would go for a walk. I would throw myself into the day. I was inspired, I was calm; calm as good suburban turf and every bit as green I would saunter across the Thames swinging my arms, the water swirling and sucking beneath me and the policemen down in the drowning-station arguing with each other over their mugs of sweetened tea.

As I left the gallery I heard someone calling behind me. Maybe I'd been found out. Someone was running and it was after me; as he neared I could hear he was quite short of breath. It was the assistant who had told me what was free and what wasn't when I'd first gone in. Maybe he wanted my leaflet back, completed, with the ten-word-phrase on it, modern art is important to me because. I tried quickly to think something up.

He ran strangely, his hand clenched out before him. Wait, he called as he ran. Wait. You dropped these. They fell out.

He looked desperate and pleased, filled with terrible import, like a messenger bringing good news about a medieval battle in a play or a film. I felt in my pocket for my wallet, but it was there. I wondered what else it was I could have dropped. I looked to see.

His hand was full of broken leaves and seeds with unlikely wings.

the heat of the story

It was midwinter. Everything was dead.

Three women came in late to Midnight Mass, their stilettos tapping on the flagstones halfway through the first reading. They came up the aisle slim-hoofed and coughing like winter deer.

They crushed with no apologies into a pew that was already packed with people. They were drunk; you could tell it. You could smell it five rows away, alcohol and worn perfume. One was young, one was older than her, and one was older than both of them. The too-bright, half-unbuttoned clothes of the youngest one were useless for this time of year, or for any time of year; the orange and metallic-blue raw and her neck and shoulder bare; and all three women dishevelled in the same liquid happiness, leaning up against one another, stamping their feet and rubbing their hands warm. Noise rose off them and hung sheer as nylon in the high roof cavity of the church over the heads of the good-coated congregation.

The woman in the middle lit a cigarette. She remembered where she was and was truly shocked at herself and dropped it. It rolled under the kneeling pad and lay there smoking itself, and when she bent down to get it back she caused the whole row of people to buckle and had to be hauled up, off balance, by the other two, before she could grind the cigarette out on the linoleum with the pointed toe of her shoe. This set all three snuffling with laughter through the Gospel, choking it back as the ageing priest read out the story one more time; no room at the inn, the terrified shepherds surrounded in light, the great throng of the heavenly host praising God and singing.

Then they sang the descant to O Come All Ye Faithful in all the wrong verses, when no one else in the church was singing the descant.

At the Sign of Peace the three women were polite and suppressed as they shook hands with the uneasy people in front of and behind them. They threw their arms around each other to wish each other peace. Though actually believe it or not the three of them had only just met that evening you know, as the half-dressed one, the youngest, was telling the man standing next to her in a voice blunt and large with drink, so unintentionally loud that the people right at the front could hear, before she flung her arms around the man's neck to give him a Christmas kiss of peace. Then, when the Mass was over and it was time to sing, too high, Hark

The Herald Angels, one of them sang the words *offspring of a virgin's wum*, to rhyme with *late in time behold him come*, and laughter and anger broke out all round them. Regulars, smiling, outraged or oblivious, who passed the women on their way out at the end, had to step over or guide their children round the legs of the youngest flung out into the aisle with one tortuous-looking shoe dangling off her foot as she lay flat out on the seat with her eyes closed, her head in the lap of the woman in her thirties who, if they stared, coolly wished them a very merry Christmas and a happy New Year, while the eldest, in her fifties, or maybe her forties, hard to tell, thanked them with her slurred eyes and smile for not standing on the girl's legs.

The priest came back through from the sacristy to find the church empty except for the women. Now they were right up at the front, dangerously close to the altar. Two of them were crouched in front of it at the side of the crib. The third was round the back of the altar waving something in the air, and as the priest came closer he could see that one of the altar boys, who was following her, rubbing his reddened neck and giggling, had let her have his long metal-tipped stick and was explaining to her how to reach up and extinguish the high candles burning round the walls.

The two at the crib-side were bent low over the plaster figures of Mary, Joseph and the baby Jesus. They were rearranging the flowers next to the Holy Family. The priest saw one of them pushing a pursed red-veined lily-head through the legs of the standing Joseph.

Now now, girls, he said.

Then he threw the women out.

Can I not finish the candles? I've those six still to do, one said.

The boy'll do that, the priest said. Give him back the stick. Let go, now.

It's freezing out there, Father. We've nowhere to go, the second said.

And Father, besides. This one's pregnant, the last said with her arm around the shoulders of the youngest woman. You can't throw her out. She's about to give birth, honest to God she is. Look.

The woman pulled up the girl's top. The old priest squinted at the bare midriff, flat and pale with cold. Its button was pierced.

If she's about to give birth then so am I, by God, he said, and herded them between the open doors. They crowded back at him. He shut one of the doors, thudding a bolt into the stone floor.

Men will soon be able to have babies, the girl was saying. I saw it on the Discovery channel.

But she is, Father, she is, the eldest of the three said. Aren't you, love? And she's got nowhere to go. Tell him, Diane.

I am, Father, it's true. I'm about to be a mother, any minute now, and we've nowhere to go. Can we not sleep in the church for the night?

You don't look in the least expecting to me, the priest said.

It can't be seen by the naked eye, the girl said. It's a phantom pregnancy.

She's giving birth to a ghost, Father, the other said.

A holy ghost, the girl said. It needs to be kept in a church.

She's full of the holy spirits, the third said.

The priest spoke through the narrow crack before he shut the door. Go home to your families, now, he said.

He turned a key in a lock. They could hear his footsteps fade away into the church still warm from all the people, and a moment later they heard the last car in the car park behind the church, parents taking the altar boy home. The boy had stood behind the priest at the door laughing shyly at their jokes. The youngest woman had tousled his hair, the second youngest had put her hand on his shoulder by his neck and the eldest had beamed at him. His face had flushed with pleasure and heat. Now the car engine stalled, stalled again, then revved up against the cold and tailed away into the night.

The women stood swaying outside the shut door. Their breath came out of them, visible.

The eldest was called Etta. The middle one's name was Moira. The youngest was Diane.

They helped each other across the road, under the railing and down the side of the riverbank. The river was high and the grass they sat on was frosty. The middle one took out her lighter, lit a cigarette. They lit the candle the youngest one had stolen. It was still freezing, though now there was almost no wind.

Still the night, the youngest said.

Aye, it is still the night, the eldest said looking at the sky. There'll be a worse frost by tomorrow, she said.

Listen to this, the middle one said. This is true. I swear it. There was this woman.

What woman, the eldest said. Someone we know?

No, look, the middle one said.

What's she called? the eldest said. Where does she work?

Listen, the middle one said. Someone told me. This is what she did. Her man died and she went and sat on his grave every night for a year. That's God's honest truth.

Like that dog in Edinburgh, the eldest said.

The youngest let herself fall backwards. Grass that had been frozen hard rasped next to her ears. Every night? she said. For a whole year? Three hundred and sixty-five nights. Sixty-six, if it was a leap year. She sat up. Why? she said. Did she think he'd come up and say hello?

I don't know, the middle one said. How would I know?

How did she get past the gateman every night? the youngest said. Did they not lock the cemetery at nights? Did she ever take a night off? Did she take her supper with her? Or did she have it every night before she went out?

I don't know, the middle one said. *I* don't know what she had for her bloody supper.

Kippers, the eldest said.

What happened after the year was up? the youngest said.

Sometimes you just feel like them, the eldest said. I don't have them very often, but tonight I just felt like them.

For Christ's sake, the middle one was saying. It's just a story.

They sat, silent. The cold of the river roared in their ears.

Listen to this, though, the eldest said. This is true as well. Because my mother used to tell me this. She's dead now. But you know how this is Christmas Eve? And how tomorrow's Christmas Day?

True enough, the middle one said. Her cigarette had gone out. She held the end of it to the candle, then put it in her mouth and sucked. It still wasn't lit.

Listen, the eldest one said. Things used to happen at midnight of the night before Christmas. Laugh if you like. But I'm telling you. My mother lived in the country when she was a girl. On Christmas Eve at midnight, back then, in the country, you could be standing at a crossroads and you could maybe hear voices.

What voices? the youngest said.

Telling you things, the eldest said nodding her head.

What things? the middle one said.

Things that could happen, the eldest said.

Did your mother actually see these voices? the middle one asked.

No, the eldest said. Because if there was water in a well it could turn into wine. But if you saw this happen, listen, you'd to look away, you'd not to look at it, or otherwise you'd be dead within the year.

All that wine, and wasted, the middle one said.

Within the year, the youngest said. That's only a week. That's not very long. Or was it within, like, the new year? like, the next year, the year coming?

Within the year, that's what she always said, the eldest said with her eyes closed.

Seven days, the youngest said. The middle one shook her head.

The eldest was shaking with cold, even in her coat. And sometimes, she said, the water could turn to blood, not wine. But it was the same. If you actually saw this happen, the wine or the blood in your well or your spring, the water changed, you'd be gone within the year.

What about a river, the youngest said. Could that change?

All three of them looked down at the river, high and speeding.

And see that priest in that church, the eldest said. I'm telling you. This *is* true. That old woman MacKinnon works for him, she's worked for him since I was a girl, and I'll bet you six hundred pounds, I'd bet you all six hundred of them, he's in her bed in there tonight.

She turned, swayed a hand towards the orange glow burning in the upstairs window in the house built on to the church.

I hope so, for his sake, the middle one said. She was shivering now too. It's bloody cold the night, she said.

Christmas, after all, the eldest said pushing her hands further up inside the cuffs of the coat.

There was one year I got a slinky, the youngest said.

A slinky what? the eldest said. The middle one laughed.

Just slinky, the youngest said. You know. They went down the stairs by themselves.

The middle one was stiff with laughter. The eldest looked bewildered.

It's a spring kind of thing, the youngest said. I was playing with it on the stairs and National Velvet was on, about Elizabeth Taylor in the race on her horse. It's an old film, she's still a child in it. It was all bright reds and browns.

Those films from before were actually brighter colours, the middle one said. They were enhanced. Technicolor.

She's been through it, that Liz Taylor, the eldest said.

She looks like she has, the middle one said.

She won the National. She cut off all her hair, the youngest said.

What if you lived in a bungalow, and you got a slinky for Christmas? the middle one said.

The eldest watched them laughing.

One time, she said. This was not long after the war either, so God knows where he got it from. My father. This wicker trunk full of fruit, he came in with it under his arm, all the cold came in round him, he put it down on the kitchen floor. My mother's face, I'm telling you. There were fruits in the basket we couldn't have imagined if we'd tried. There were fruits I've never seen the like of since.

Can you remember what they tasted like? the middle one said.

To this day, the eldest said.

Like eating technicolor, the youngest said.

The eldest nodded.

The other two have gone, one running and the other limping, both chasing a light on the top of a car in case it was a taxi. There's just her left. The middle one gave her a ten pound note. The other gave her her coat, and she's wearing it now. It's wet all up the back from the ground, and the shoulders and arms are still the shape of the older woman, but they're warm from her. I'll not need it, the woman had said taking it off and letting it drop as she went. You'll need it more. We're getting that taxi.

She looks up. The sky is covered in stars, like white stubble.

The older one has a sick father. That'd be one of the reasons she didn't want to go home too soon. The other one didn't seem to have any reason to not want to go home. It could be anything.

She hopes the two women are on their way home to houses that are warm.

She grips her way up the riverbank slope. Below her on the grass are three small dark places where the frost has scuffed away and melted, the places where the three of them were sitting talking. Her head is clearer now, less misty. Earlier, things were moving round her head by themselves, like shapes in a fog. Now they've settled down. She sees the church across the road, dismal in the street light. She remembers. They went in there to get warmed up.

It makes her laugh. Now when she goes past that church she can think to herself, I've been inside there and put out the candles on Christmas Eve. And there was the old priest too, who threw them out, but not till the end. The man next to her in the row, the one she kissed. All the people from the church tonight, wrapped up for Christmas like rich presents, listening to the old story about a birth in the middle of winter. As if, on Christmas morning, they could open their front doors and find themselves delivered to themselves new-born on their own doorsteps, in a basket like those exotic fruits, or in one of those wine boxes made of expensive wood and full of straw.

She follows the bend of the river. Round the corner and down the street the lights of the city are still on, though most of the city is home by now, asleep, waiting. The altar boy; he'll be asleep in a small bed somewhere over there with the covers up to his neck and the central heating set to come on by itself in the morning. All over town, all the people sealed with sleep into houses whose roofs, sheened with white just now, will be blackened again where the sun hits them in the morning. And that woman, the one on the grave of the dead man. If she's on the grave tonight she's wearing a big sheepskin and gloves and a scarf, and has one of those heaters that campers take on holiday with them, and the heat coming off it is lighting up the cemetery and its trees, all their branches bare and iced, evergreen and iced.

There's sand on the pavement. She can feel it under her feet. Above her, frost and empty sky. She reaches up and shakes frost off a branch of the tree next to the parking machine. The branch in her hand is all tight closed buds. She lets it flick back up and frost crystals fling off all round the tree, like water off a dog.

The clock on the parking machine is covered in frost lit up from behind. She rubs at it with her cold hand. Two forty-six a.m. She leans on the rail and listens. Nothing but the river, and far away at the back of it some people shouting and singing, celebrating. She wraps the coat closed around her and puts her hands in its pockets. A burnt-down candle; a ten pound note; someone else's random crumbs and dust.

She starts walking, anywhere, she doesn't know where.

The street is deserted, except for a man coming towards her on the other side of the road. He is out walking two small Jack Russell dogs in the dark at three o'clock on Christmas morning.

There's a story in that, she thinks as they pass each other by.

It's too dark to see his face. Merry Christmas, love, he calls across the road to her. Have a good one.

The words are full of thaw.

Merry Christmas, she tells him back. All the best.

the start of things

It was the end and we both knew it.

What'll we do about it? you said.

I shrugged. I can't imagine, I said.

You shook your head. Me neither, you said.

We stood useless in the living room. Its furniture was pointless. I realized I was standing as if waiting politely for you to leave. You were waiting too, poised and formal, as if you had just got to your feet to wish a guest goodbye.

I crossed my arms. You put your hands on your hips.

There were black smudges round your eyes as if you hadn't slept for weeks. I knew I had the same dark round my own. Outside it was sleeting, the evening was bitterly cold; it was the worst month of the year, the one where the days seem darker, the weeks seem longer, the money seems to take longer to reach people's bank accounts.

I sat down on the couch. You sat down next to me.

Though the central heating was turned up as high as it would go, the house still seemed to be full of holes. We both stared at the empty hearth in the wall.

You know what? you said.

What? I said.

We could maybe start a fire, you said.

Yes, I said.

I went to get the matches from the bedroom while you took today's newspaper apart. Then I went out into the sleet to get the logs from the shed. I chose smaller ones as well as a couple of larger ones and then carefully selected a large wet log from the pile outside the shed and balanced it on top of the load because, as you always say, a wet log burns really well on a good fire. But when I came up the garden the back door was shut and wouldn't open. I put the logs down. I tried the handle again.

I knocked. I knocked harder.

I picked up the biggest and heaviest of the logs and hammered the door hard with it. Woodlice and spiders and bits of rotten wood jolted off the log. Mossy slime smeared the door and came off all up my hands and sleeves. I took a step back and smashed at the door again. You opened the top part of the kitchen window a tiny crack.

There's no other way to do this, you said through the crack.

You cheap bastard, I said.

Stop it, you said. You'll damage the door.

You bet I'll damage the fucking door, I said. It's my

door. I can damage it if I want. And if you don't open it right now I'll break all my windows as well.

It's my house, you said, and shut the window and locked it. We had had those locks put on by a joiner to deter burglars. I could see you behind the condensation. You were by the kettle, you were pretending I wasn't there. Steam was coming out of the kettle. You opened the fridge and took out the milk. It was me who'd bought that milk; I had bought it at the shop the day before and you just using it like that made me angrier than anything else. I stood in the rainy sleet and shouted and swore. You acted like you couldn't hear. You took a teabag pensively out of a box as if I didn't exist, as if I had never existed, as if I were mere audience to you, out in the dark with the rest of the masses watching you, the star of the film, meaningfully making a cup of tea.

I picked up the biggest log again, swung it up to shoulder height, got my footing and aimed it right at you. But our kitchen windows are double glazed, we had them redone last year when all the wood round the old windows was rotting, and the new glass we'd had put in is reinforced. I didn't want to look stupid, throwing a log that would just bounce off again. I let the log drop back on to the stones.

Now it was sleeting from all directions; there were slices of wet sleet stuck all over me, in my hair, on my jumper, down the back of my neck. A splinter of sleet was melting on my face. I wiped it off. I couldn't really feel my hands any more. I had no gloves or jacket, I had nothing, no money or bank cards or phone. Everything I needed was in the house. I thought of my coat and scarf, hanging so simple and so unhaveable on the hook by the front door. I was freezing. I hugged myself. I couldn't even go and sit in the car. The car keys were in my coat pocket. All I had was the shed key. In a minute, if I got any colder, I was going to have to go and stand in the shed.

Then I realized that since I had the key for the shed I probably also had the spare front door key, which we always keep on the same keyring, the keyring that's got the small world globe on it. I put my hand in my pocket; there it was, the world on the chain and both its keys attached, and in the same fraction of a second (I could see it in the way you turned at the sideboard and stopped with the cup in your hand) the thought that I might have these keys entered your head; at the very same moment that I started for the front of the house I saw out of the corner of my eye the moment of you in mid air darting forward to get there first.

It was a race. I ran the best I could, but the ground under my feet was slippery. When I reached the front, my heart beating hard and high, I was just in time to hear it, the click of the double lock and you, the winner, triumphant behind the door. You were laughing. It made me want to laugh too. Then the beginning of wanting to laugh made me want to cry.

There was no way in the world I was going to cry in front of you, even if you were on the other side of a door and couldn't see me. In the light from the living-room window I worked the spare front door key off the keyring. This was quite hard to do because the ring of the keyring is quite tight and my fingers were so cold I could hardly move them. When I'd finally got it free I lifted the letterbox cover and posted the key through the door. I heard the lightness of it hit the mat. I heard your laughing stop. I let the cover fall shut and I turned my back and went.

We are in bed with our backs to one another. The wind is howling on the roof and battering at the cardboard taped over the broken window. I can still smell the fire; the smell of it is all through the house, like some ash-scented animal has slunk muskily about, marking its territory in all the rooms.

We are inches away from each other. I can feel the reach of each inch. In the end I give in and begin.

Remember the time you didn't come home all night, I say, the time I hadn't a clue where you were and I thought you were dead?

You laugh gently behind me in the dark.

I'm sorry, you say.

No, it was good, I say. It was good to see the morning like that. It was the spring, remember?

Actually, you say, I was just thinking about the time last summer that you fell in love and it wasn't with me.

Ah, I say. I laugh. I hope the laugh sounds wry and apologetic.

No, it was good too, you say, it was really good, you know it was, it was good for both of us. I mean, I

know it was good for you, and for me personally, well I
found out all sorts of new things.

Like what? I say.

I really don't know, you say.

No? I say.

No, I mean that's what I found out, you say. I found
out what it means not to know.

Like that time we were in the Underground, I say,
and the train doors shut and I was still on the platform
right behind you and you got on the train and the doors
closed before I could get in?

I remember, you say behind me.

And we were miming at each other through the
doors of the train, I say, and then the train began to
move and you were saying something through the glass
but I had absolutely no idea what it was you were
trying to tell me.

Embankment, you say. I was telling you
Embankment. I wanted us to meet at Embankment.

But I had no idea what the word could be, I say,
there was just your mouth making this shape over and
over and I couldn't hear what it was, then your carriage
all lit up going into the dark and all the other carriages
going after it with all the people in them, and then just
the opening of the tunnel and nothing but the adverts
for alcohol and airline companies and below them the
rails, always so shining, like the fact that they're
dangerous seems to be something to do with the way
they shine, and I was standing there and I couldn't
imagine at all what it was you'd been trying to tell me,

I was making the shape of it with my own mouth but the only word I could think of that fitted the shape was the word ombudsman.

We are both laughing by now. We turn in the warm space we've made in the bed. I feel your breath on me in the dark as you say it.

Ombudsman, you say.

Ombudsman, for God's sake, I say. I didn't even know what it meant. I still don't. I couldn't think of any reason why you would ever want to say it to me. So I thought it must be, it has to be, another word. Then I thought that maybe it was the word embarrassment.

Embarrassment, you say. Yes. Let's meet at Embarrassment station. I'll be waiting for you at Embarrassment.

Because it had been a bit embarrassing, I say, what with the people on the train and on the platform seeing the doors close on us and everything, so it could have been embarrassment. Then I thought that maybe what you'd been telling me was two words, not one. Something like embarrass me, or embrace me. And then there was nobody left on the platform except me, it was all different people waiting for another train, and then their train came in and they got on and people got off and I was still standing there on the platform talking to myself, going embarrass me, no, embrace me, no, employ me, no.

We laugh towards each other. Then we're silent again and I have no idea where it is you've gone to

inside your head. I wonder if you're thinking of that
night you didn't come home. I think about my other
love, then how I'm standing on that platform, the
trains coming and going one after the other, the people
and the dead air in the Underground shifting round me
each time, and each time I'm wondering should I get
the next one and go to the next station along the line to
see if maybe you're there waiting for me? But what if I
get there and you aren't? Worse, what if I go somewhere
else but you're on a train on your way back to find me?
Perhaps, I think, I should go back to the café we've just
been in. Or perhaps it would be sensible to go to one of
our favourite places, the diner, or the place where all
the roads meet and the flower shop is, or the Chinese
place, or the restaurant with the rooftop views, and
wait for you there. Or if all else fails I could go back to
the main station and catch the train home.

But all I can think to do, and all I really want to do,
is close my eyes and sink down till I'm on the ground
there on the grimy platform, because all round me for
miles is the old cave of the Underground and above and
beyond it the city in winter, a city I thought I knew,
only now it's as nondescript as sea and me a stone
tossed into it going down to its colourless floor.

The house creaks round us. I lean against you in the
bed. The bed creaks. You lean back hard against me
and it fills me with a hope so open that I'm scared to
acknowledge it. I can still smell fire and embers; tonight
I can smell the season the way it's usually only possible
to at the very first moments of its return, before you're

used to it, when you've forgotten its smell, then there it is back in the air and the flow of things shifting and resettling again.

I put my nose against your skin. You smell of you. You always smell of you, though there are, I know, variations on the scent of you; the summer smell of deep leaves and sweat, the autumn smell of smokiness, the winter smell of fire and clean worn wool, the spring smell I can't remember exactly and am waiting to know again.

You lean down and speak by my ear.

Embankment me, you say. You say it as quietly as breathing.

What? I say.

Embarrass me, you say.

Okay, I whisper. I will if you embalm me.

I will, you whisper back. But only if you imbue me. And would you like me to imbue you?

Yes, I say. Please. Start now.

The key hit the mat and I stopped laughing.

I stood by the front door and listened.

I tried to check through the window. I couldn't see anything but my own reflection and the reflection of the room behind me. I went round the room switching off all the lamps and then back to the window to try to see through it.

I went into the kitchen again to get my cup of tea. I stood in the kitchen for a while holding the cup. I came back through the dining room and the living room and went upstairs, where I carried the cup from room to room. I tried to look as if I meant to do this though there was nobody to see whether I did or didn't; the rooms were all empty. You were out there with no coat. The weather was filthy. I opened the bedroom window. The sleeting had stopped; I looked up and down the road. There was nothing but wet cars parked outside houses.

I shut the window and locked it. The fact that I was worrying about you when you so clearly weren't even thinking about me, wherever you were, annoyed me. All round me in the room there was nothing but things. That hairbrush on the dresser was mine but the hair-dryer, which we both use, was definitely yours. The dresser was mine; it had belonged to my mother. The bed was ours. The duvet was yours. I went to sit in the bathroom, the room with the least number of things in it. I looked at the empty bath. Its surface has been badly in need of re-enamelling ever since we bought this house.

I would go downstairs now, I thought as I sat there, and look up bath enamellers in the Yellow Pages and tomorrow I would phone people up for estimates. That was what life was about, keeping things well and running, flowing and in good order, the homefires burning. That was what survival was about, re-enamelling the bath even when other seemingly more important things had reached their end.

But the Yellow Pages wasn't in the place where we usually keep it. I couldn't imagine where it was. I went round and round the downstairs rooms looking for it, because you had taken it from where it's meant to be kept, where we agreed to always put it after we'd finished using it, you had selfishly taken it and left it somewhere completely impossible for me to find and you had probably done it on purpose, you were always doing things like that, taking things from where they're supposed to be and leaving them somewhere else. You had taken the Yellow Pages in the full knowledge that I would need it and then you had not just carelessly but completely callously left it somewhere I would never think in a million years to look.

I got angrier and angrier. I stood in the kitchen. I opened cupboard doors and slammed them closed again. As I left the kitchen, slapping at the light switch with the palm of my hand to conserve energy, I noticed the weak light in the shed window.

I nearly tripped on a pile of logs you had left right by the back door. I could have done myself an injury if I'd fallen on them, I told myself as I stamped out across the slippery grass.

You were in the shed. I could see you through the cobwebbed window. I saw as I got closer that you were wearing round your shoulders and over your head the blankets we use for sitting on the grass in the summer. You looked ridiculous. You had one hand out of the blankets holding an old torch in the air. In the wavering battery light of it I saw you were reading a book.

The shed door was held shut with something, maybe

the lawnmower. I pushed against it and it wouldn't give. I rapped hard on the window.

What did you do with the Yellow Pages? I shouted.

I rapped again.

I need the Yellow Pages, I shouted.

You turned your head slowly. You settled the blankets round you and turned back to the book as if you'd glanced out of a moving window in a train or a car at something and it had been of no interest to you.

That's when it flashed into my head exactly where the Yellow Pages was. It was where it had been for months, randomly open on the back seat of the car; we had fetched it from the house a couple of months ago when you said you'd teach me to drive, because, you'd said, I could sit on it to give myself a little more height in the driver's seat.

I was embarrassed. For a moment I considered pretending to forget that I'd remembered where the Yellow Pages was so I could go on self-righteously shouting at you. But the absurdity of even considering this, and then the absurdity of you visibly shivering with cold, wrapped in blankets, reading in the shed and me jumping up and down with cold, shouting at you in the garden in the middle of winter on a pitch-black night made me want to laugh. I almost did. I had to stop myself. I stood in the cold by the spindly tree. You had shown me which pedal was which and explained to me how a clutch worked. You had taken me to the near-empty Homebase car park and let me drive round and round for an hour and you had only been angry once, only for a moment, pulling the handbrake up when I went too close to the only other car in the car park.

I thought about why I had been so angry earlier. I tried to work myself up about it again but instead I couldn't help myself, I began to wonder what book it was you were reading and if it was the book we'd left out on the bench in the garden since last August, first out of forgetfulness, then out of laziness, then finally because we were both curious about what would actually happen to a book if we left it outside in the weather. I wondered if it had warped, what it felt like in your hands. It had been out there in heat and cold and wet for months. I wondered if the pages had stuck together so that when you tried to open them the print might transfer to the opposite page and make the book unreadable, so that every time you turned a page you'd have to peel it carefully back.

Right then the wind rose and I heard the back door slam shut, but I was fine, I had my keys in my pocket. I walked the length of the garden away from the shed, went round to the front door, got my keys out and was about to put the key in the lock and let myself back in when I remembered your doorkey falling so lightly on to the mat.

I could post my own key through the door. I could go back round to the shed and tell you I was locked out too. Then we could break back in to the house together. We could go back to where this had begun. Maybe once we'd got back in we could even start the

fire you'd gone for logs for. In fact I would make a
point of fetching the logs in, to show you how I trusted
you.

I imagined myself going down the garden again and
telling you through the shed window that we were both
locked out and that I needed you. But you might
choose not to respond. If that's what you chose then I'd
break back in on my own.

Or I could just open the door right now and go into
the warm, shut the door after me, run a bath, go to bed
early and read a book for a while by myself before I fell
asleep.

I stood at the door with the key in my hand and of
course I decided yes.

0207 382
6128

Richard
Jarram

Reg 090580

(Scandal
Court
3 8 - 4?
chancll
St
Nearest
Shop
Moorgate